Frozen

CW00868503

Edward Yeoman

June 2021

Frozen Assets by Edward Yeoman

Published by Edward Yeoman

http://tvhost.co.uk

Cover by Edward Yeoman

ISBN: 9798511304519 (Paperback edition)

Imprint: Independently published

Dedication

To the divine Valerie for allowing me to tap
away on my laptop through the dark evenings!

To Mark

Enjoy your 71st
year on this wonderful
world!

Ted, x Val

Contents

June 1977

I am enjoying the feel of sunshine on my back. I am lying on a towel spread out on a sandy beach in Menorca. I decide to turn over before I burn. It is fabulous being warm, without layer upon layer of clothing.

For over two years, I had worked in the Arctic North. Norway to be precise, north of the city of Tromso; one of the most hostile environments in the world. Permanent darkness, from mid - November to mid - January. Cold; between October and April it seldom gets above freezing and it can get down to minus eighteen degrees Celsius. The nearest city was Soviet Murmansk. It wasn't as if you could just pop over the border for a few days of R and R.

What had inspired me to spend a whole year in that hellhole? Money, filthy lucre, cash, the wherewithal to be able to afford to be lying on this beach today. To be able to watch some hippy chicks scrambling over the rocks across the little inlet and playing in the sea without a care in the world and even fewer clothes. That wasn't about to happen if I had stayed in England.

June 1974

I don't understand, even now, how it had all gone so wrong. "Go to university, get a degree and a good job." That is what they had all told me, my parents, the teachers at school and even the Government. So, I did.

I'd spent three years living on a (partial) student grant. In the year before I started uni, my folks had earnt, just a little too much for me to get a full grant from the State. Then, sadly, my Dad's commission payments dried up.

*****

It was 1972 and the recession was starting to bite. I wasn't the only person having to draw their spending plans in. What with the miner's strike, unemployment and inflation rising; much of the population was going short. My Dad worked in an estate agency and people weren't buying houses. He could no longer make up the notional parental contribution. I struggled on, living on beans and toast.

Room to Let.
Shared house 1 mile to the University.
All facilities shared.
Engineering students preferred.

It went on to quote a sum for rent that I could afford. I was strapped for cash; I was on less than the full grant and had some meagre savings from a job, cleaning factories over the summer vacation. I dashed around to the address, knocked on the door and asked for James.

"That's me." The tall, well-groomed chap, maybe a few years older than me, introduced himself. "James Hesketh, are you here about the room?"

We chatted about our respective courses as he showed me the rooms, I had the first choice. Everything in the kitchen looked brand new.

"Electrical engineering for me, I couldn't face all that underground stuff!"

I could understand that: I'll admit it took all my nerve to stay in the cage as the gates clanged shut when we visited the collieries. I knew it was as safe as it could be made. People like me (after I'd graduated, of course) spend hours checking and rechecking the loads placed on the tunnel supports and other safety designs.

"The rules are pretty simple. Keep the place clean. Make a mess and you clean it up. Respect the others living here, we will all have work to do so noise, smells and drunken

4

behaviour are to be kept to a minimum. I am the name on the property so be nice to the neighbours."

Dec arrived at the front door just before I left, James introduced me to the newcomer as his housemate. I was in!

I hurried off to get my stuff from the Bed and Breakfast I'd been staying at. It was cheap because it was miles out of town. I'd taken it in desperation after having to turn down the unaffordable room in the Halls of Residence I had originally planned to take.

For the next couple of years, I had worked hard, slaving long hours in the library studying the textbooks I couldn't afford to buy. I pretty much stayed out of the politics and campaigning that students, in general, were supposed to be involved in. I just kept my head down and graduated in 1974. I had earnt myself a fairly good 2-1 degree, in mining engineering. Not that it helped.

The three of us, me, Dec and James had stayed in the house, living a comfortable shared existence for the two years needed to complete my and Dec's courses. James had another year to go when it was time for me and Dec to move on.

October 1974

In the world outside the cloistered life of academia, Sod's Law was, of course, in charge.

The lack of demand caused by the 'three-day week' meant little demand for raw products. That had forced the various mining industries into a state of contraction. Over a million people were unemployed, investment was at a low, the country was in a mess. Three months after graduating, my prospects were even worse.

It was on a lad's weekend then that I met up with Dec, my former housemate from university and his cousin from Norway, Andreas. There were any number of fishing families with ties across the North Sea, some going back centuries. It was one of the important encounters on my road to Menorca.

Andreas had money, enough to travel to Britain, enough to pay for all the beer that evening. He even paid for the chips, as we walked to the station for their train back to Leeds.

Andreas told us about the iron ore mine he worked at; he was a clerk in the production office. The place was cold and dark, "but they have good heating in the office!" He had joked.

"So, why do you work in a cold, dark place like that?" I had asked.

"Money, it pays very well indeed. I sit in a warm office and earn more than a trawlerman. I think I earn as much as the workers on the oil rigs, and I don't have to go to work by helicopter. It is better to work in Finnmark!"

A great yarn, a man reaping big rewards for braving the northern wilderness. It could have stayed like that, just a yarn. I could have found a proper job, maybe a girlfriend worthy of the appellation, but it wasn't to be.

*****

I did find a job, not the sort of thing I was hoping for as I'd laboured over essays, in the university library, at midnight, still, it was a job.

Every Monday, a van would arrive outside my parent's house. The driver would offload a pile of boxes, I'd sign for them. He went off to the next drop point. I'd take the boxes through to the dining room and empty them into three piles.

For almost every waking hour after that, I would pick up a greeting card, an envelope and slide them into a cellulose sleeve, fold over the top and secure it with a sticky label. Then repeat. Thousands of times.

On Friday evening, the van would draw up, the driver would check and count the boxes of packaged cards. He would fill out a chitty, while I loaded the boxes into the van. He kept the top copy of the chitty and the carbon copy was handed to me.

"A good weeks work! Take this to the office before noon tomorrow and they'll pay you what's owing."

It was just there was never enough owing. I gave my Mum half of it, for the housekeeping. The rest, after I had bought a record, went in a jar in my bedroom.

"Why don't you go out with some of your friends?" Mum asked.

"Yeah, spend an exciting evening moaning about having no money and trying to make a half last two hours. What's the point? I might as well watch another Panorama report on the diminishing coal industry." That shut her up.

I went to my room, closed the door, and hated myself for being so cruel.

*****

I spent several of my hours in that room trying to reconcile my vague hippy, pacifist views, love and peace man, smash violence! With the knowledge that James my other housemate from university, an officer in the Royal Engineers, was making good money. Not that he lacked money as a student.

*****

"If I can't find good people like you for next year, I might just live alone and pay the mortgage myself." He had told Dec and me as we packed our bags.

"Pay the mortgage yourself, James?"

"If someone doesn't the Building Society will want it back!"

"You mean to say you own this house?" Dec was as surprised as me.

"My Mother gave me the deposit, but yes". Then the whole story had come out.

James Alexander Hesketh-Stuart, or should I say, Lieutenant James Alexander Hesketh-Stuart, of the Royal Engineers, had been our landlord the whole time. That explained the comparatively low rent we had been asked for.

"Mates rates".

He had bought, refitted and redecorated the house when the Army had signed him off to do a degree. He was also being paid by the Army and in return he was subject to military discipline. That explained the short hair and smarter than the average student appearance.

It also explained how he managed to maintain his relationship with Lindsey. Both Dec and I had recognised very quickly, that as charming and friendly as she was, girls like Lindsey were not of our social milieu.

*****

Try as I might, I couldn't get past the abhorrence of the thought of being called on to kill another person. The thought of sending other men to their possible death … No that was way beyond me.

November 1974

I was still stuffing cards in bags when one morning, about a month later, Andreas phoned. He had been in Leeds visiting his cousin, Dec again.

"The beer is so much cheaper than Norway. I think I save money by drinking in Britain, even after paying my ferry fare!" He explained.

"Great," I failed to enthuse. I hadn't even had the chance to turn down a weekend on the lash, I'd not been invited.

"I have to suddenly return to Norway; my Mother has been taken to hospital. I have a seat on an aeroplane tomorrow morning. It leaves very early, I cannot get from Dec's house in time, in the morning. Is it possible for me to spend the night at your house? It is much closer to London Airport?"

Well, what could I say? "Yes, of course, what time do I expect you?"

"I was thinking about five hours, is that good? Then we can have a good bevvy and a laugh before bed!"

'Five hours?' My brain raced and my schoolboy German kicked in, 'Fünf Uhr! Five o'clock.' "Yes, Andreas, five o'clock is good for me, I will meet you at the railway station."

"Can you not meet me at the bus station, I come by coach!"

"The coach station, no problem." I'd have to see if I could borrow the Mini from my Mum.

*****

We had a good night out too. Several pints at the Queen's Head, before we walked to the curry house. There I persuaded Andreas to try a little of my madras style curry, alongside the cooler biryani that Dec had introduced him to. It might have been too early in his curry training. We ordered another round of lagers to cool his taste buds.

"Wait until you come to Norway, I will get you to try some Rakfisk, sadly the beer is too expensive to use to clean your mouth!"

"Sadly, I don't think I can afford to come to Norway, Andreas. I told you about my job." I took another swig of the lager to get the bitter taste of failure out of my mouth.

"Of course, you can!" Andreas laughed. "You can have my return ticket for the ferry.

When you arrive, I will take you to Bjørnevatn and I will get you a job in mining!"

"A job? Just like that?"

"Yes, it is a hard life, like fishing, the oil rigs and forestry. There are only so many men in Norway willing to do this work. At the moment, all the glamour is in working on the drilling platforms in the Nord See."

"North…" I began to correct his pronunciation and stopped. This could be it. My big chance, my ticket out of here, being offered to me by a half-drunken Norwegian. A man I had met once before. There was only one problem.

"But …" I could feel my hopes fading, my optimism falling. "I don't speak any Norwegian!".

"You have some German; you will get by. I will help you." Andreas grinned. "Besides, many Norwegians speak some English. We learn it from the Beatles' records and Hollywood Movies!"

*****

In the morning, I drove Andreas to the Airport. I bade him farewell and expressed my hopes that his mother would recover.

15

"If it is worse, I will phone you! Otherwise, I will meet you off the ferry next weekend."

I drove home, with the return half of a ferry ticket to Norway in my pocket. What were my folks going to say?

"Iron ore mining? In Norway?"

"Yes, Mum." She looked at my Dad, who was sat on the opposite side of the supper table. Something passed between them.

"Son, you have no idea how hard the work is going to be, nor how cold it gets in winter up there. Have you?"

"No, Dad, not really but Andreas manages and James has been there on exercise and came back to tell the tales." James had spent two weeks the previous winter on Exercise Northern Cold.

"Ski-school for us duffers! It was great with the right gear!" I'd phoned James last night and talked about Norway. "I don't know much about the country; we were in barracks or hiding in snow holes most of the time. So, I didn't get to speak to many locals. Sorry, I can't be more helpful."

"If it doesn't work out?"

"It has to Dad; I can't do the greetings cards forever!"

"You need to have a contingency plan. James will have told you about them!"

"Yes, Dad. He has and I have one." I pause, wondering how to present this. "Mum, I want you to keep my savings, nearly fifty quid, and if it all goes to pot, you can use it to buy me a ticket home."

Mum placed her hand on mine. I must have missed another one of the silent messages passing between my parents. My Dad coughed, clearing his throat.

"Son, we wish you the best of luck. I am so proud of you for refusing to lie down and be walked over. Go to Norway, make your fortune and if you don't, we'll make sure you get home!"

I don't say it often enough, but in that moment I realised that I loved my parents, because they loved me, unconditionally.

December 1974

Let me make it clear, it was like working in hell. It was heavy, exhausting, physical work. Long shifts and short breaks. We lived in a barrack block that made the University Halls of Residence look like a four-star hotel.

Outside, we worked under electric arc light morning, noon and … It was night, always night. It was cold, very cold, we were wrapped up in special suits with no skin exposed. Standing still for too long or holding something metal in your gloved hand for longer than a few minutes, put you at risk of frostbite.

Gloves made it hard to control tools. Hoods dampened the sounds around you. Goggles restricted your peripheral vision. Face masks muffled instructions and muted warning shouts.

"As cold as Hell and twice as dangerous." As the instructor doing my safety lecture repeated several times.

Soon it was the spring. The sun was starting to appear low on the horizon, at first for a few minutes. Then it was a few hours, I knew soon it would not set. This changing light was messing with my sleep patterns. I was soon relying on the plentiful meals, not only for sustenance, but to regulate my body clock. If it hadn't been for James' advice I would have quit.

*****

"You will have to set yourself a target. Something that you can think of and say, 'When I have reached, whatever it is, all this will be worthwhile.' That will help you keep going. Except I wouldn't have got through my Army Officer Training Course at Sandhurst if that had been my only target." James had paused, I guessed he was remembering some incident. "Yep, it was smaller ones, the daily targets that kept me in there. One time I nearly quit." That surprised me. I decided not to comment. "I made up my mind that I would allow myself to drop out if I didn't finish the run the next day. I started out aiming to reach the first checkpoint. I was OK when I got there, so I aimed for the next one and before I knew it I was at the finish line. Complete phase one, phase two and eventually I was on the Parade Ground, the Parents watching as I graduated."

"So, James, you reckon I should set an endpoint and lots of little reward points on the way?" I sought confirmation.

"Exactly!"

*****

I was working four weeks on, one week off, five days a week. Except I didn't. I was working five days on, one day overtime and one day off each week. I liked having the money piling into my account and what was there for me to do with time off?

Unlike the rest of my work crew, I didn't trek into town to have a drink. Certainly not at the prices they talked about having to pay. The other big draw for off-shift miners was sex. However, I was too scared to visit the whore house. Supposing I caught something awful!

The week I had arrived, they had sacked a group of men for failing drug tests. Safety was important to management. A death or serious injury would shut the mine down for days while it was investigated. There was no tolerance of drugs or drunkenness.

That explained the need to get to town for a beer, the site was dry. So that was sex and drugs and booze out of scope.

I wasn't interested in losing my money in card games or other forms of gambling either. I was here to earn enough to be able to afford some of my dreams.

On my first week off, I spent three days getting home and two getting back, but I did it. I took my Mum and Dad out for dinner. Not just a meal out, we ate at the 'Il Luogo Restaurant',

21

the place to eat in the area. I paid cash. It felt so good that I allowed Dad to pay for our taxi home.

"I won't be back for a few months," I had informed them as I packed my small bag. "There are other places I want to visit while I have the chance!"

"Don't forget to put a little away for the future, Son!" My Mum had reminded me at the front door. "As lovely as Il Luogo was, you have a long life ahead of you!"

"I won't forget, Mum. It is why I am working in distant Norway after all!" I pecked her on the cheek. Then hugged Dad, in a 'manly' sort of way, and set off to the station and all points North.

March 1975

Several weeks later, I found myself sitting on the terrace of a café in Montmartre, sipping one of those tiny cups of coffee. Yes! Me in Paris in the (very mild) Spring.

'Score another dream,' I thought, as I watched two young Mademoiselles chat animatedly about something, laughing and imitating someone I would never meet's gestures and expressions. So chic, so Parisienne, so close to how I had imagined it being.

I had another very good reason for visiting Paris that weekend and that was securely zipped into my jacket pocket. Following advice from one or two of the guys I'd talked to, I'd just opened an account with Credit Suisse. Every month, the bank I used in Norway would transfer two-thirds of my Norwegian Krona to Credit Suisse. Credit Suisse would then convert it into Swiss Francs.

The Krona was fixed at twenty to the pound, but the value of the Swiss Franc just seemed to keep going up against the pound. It made sense to speculate against the pound. It was another way to build up the value of my savings. I could just tell that a new wave of industrial inaction would hit British industry very soon and that would spell more trouble for the British economy. The balance of payments, the trade deficit and the value of the pound abroad were all heading for a rough ride.

April 1975

I next time I went home it was the week after Easter. I had arranged to meet up with Dec and James. Andreas was taking the same flight to England. He had met a young lady and was keen to spend as much time with her as possible. Between us, we had decided that five days travel for a few hours with people we cared about was a good use of our time. We had bitten the bullet and booked flights.

I didn't see Andreas often in Norway. The office complex doors were kept shut against the cold and the outside workers were discouraged from entering.

"Part of that is because it takes nearly an hour for an outsider to get undressed and then back into their kit. A very poor use of a worker's time." Andreas had explained, as we got comfortable in our seats aboard the train to Tromso.

"That makes sense," I dozed off.

We were waiting for our flight before I was ready to restart our conversation. I had shed my bulky, puffy, parka jacket. Not so much because it was hot, it was at the same temperature as normal. Great insulation but it made me move like the Michelin Man. Andreas was still wearing his sheepskin jacket and shivering.

"What was it you were saying about getting outdoor kit off and back on?" I tried to tease him.

"You'll find out!"

I didn't get much more out of him.

"Too much risk of getting your hopes up, but Andreas is working for you!"

*****

James and Dec, Declan as I had to call him now, were both in good form.

"I'm Mr Declan at work now, Deputy Fleet Engineering Manager!" He had boasted.

"How are other things going? I hear they have some new rowing boats on the lake now too." James sniped back.

"Alright, it is not the biggest fleet in the North Sea, but we have four trawlers at sea, one unloading in Stavanger and another in dock at Immingham, where we are having to repair some damage. She got into a squabble with some Icelandic boats."

Dec had done well, his family connections with some of the big names in the fishing industry had helped. On the other hand, there were lots of Marine Engineers out there. Dec had got a foot on the ladder and was climbing it.

James was about to graduate and with it get a promotion to a "two pip" Lieutenant. What was I doing?

"I opened a Swiss Bank account." Well, it was true.

"Yeah, Andreas, did you meet my cousin, James?" A shake of the head. "He works at the same place, he says they think highly of our ugly friend in the North!"

"Probably because it is dark and too cold for him to unzip his trousers!" James threw out a veiled, well no so veiled, observation about my sex life. "I certainly wouldn't want my bits out in temperatures that low!"

An element of respect? I doubted it and braced for the follow up that never came.

"Another beer? Or do we head for a curry?"

What had got into Dec, normally he would be talking about a few more bevvies and heading to a night club. He must have seen the look on my face.

"I promised Mary, I'd be home before midnight and only slightly the worse for drink!"

Mary had been mentioned in several of Dec's letters. The last had suggested that they might be moving in together. It appeared things had moved on since it was written.

"How is your love life, James? Still being beastly towards the lovely Lindsey?"

"I try my best." He paused, a longer pause than usual, a significant pause. "I would like you to block the last Saturday of June next year in your diaries!"

"It's not his Graduation, that's this year." Dec started the wind-up.

"It could be, we don't know if he has done any work this year!" I jumped on the bandwagon.

"The Army wouldn't like that."

"That is true too, but what else could it be, Dec?"

"Declan!"

"Sorry Mr Declan."

"It is my wedding day, Idiots!" James had decided we had gone far enough.

May 1975

Back in the now, nearly permanent, daylight of Northern Norway, I found myself in conversations with the Duty Engineer or his Deputy. Mainly they want to know how best to explain things to my colleagues with the picks and spades. Yes, we still used them, even with all the big heavy machines.

I also got drawn into a conversation with Knut, the Shift Safety Officer. Gloves. They had been essential in the deep winter. Not only did they prevent frostbite but they stopped the skin on your hands from being frozen to tools, walkway stanchions and the huge diggers. They were genuine lifesavers.

They had drawbacks though, they made picking up objects and tools almost impossible. Fine control of machines and keeping a grip on a pick shaft were much more difficult and demanding. During the cold, the clear and instant dangers made the choice to keep your gloves on very easy.

Now it was warmer, the temptation to remove the thick, insulating, impediments to pick something up, to make that minor adjustment to a knob was much greater. In the eyes of my fellow 'grunts', it was safer to remove their gloves, reach for whatever it was and grab it the first time, as opposed to fumbling with gloves on and losing sight of what was going on around them.

"It is just that these bad habits become ingrained," The Safety Officer explained. My understanding of Norwegian was getting better, *inngrodd*, ingrained. "last October, before you arrived, there were two deglovings, three amputations and a broken back, from not wearing gloves."

"Deglovings?" I had to ask.

"Where the skin is pulled off the underlying muscles and bones. Taken off like a glove." I felt my balls being retracted into my body as I assimilated the nature of this type of injury. "The broken back included a partial degloving. The guy had rested a bare hand on the bucket of a crane as he signalled to the operator to take it up. He was five maybe ten metres up before his skin tore and he fell."

"Shit!" OK, I so used another word but you get the picture.

"Yes, Shit! I don't want that to happen again this fall!"

"I see your problem but no immediate solutions. Can I think on this for a few days?"

I walked back to my shovel with an appointment, in an office, inside the admin building. Was this what Andreas had been hinting at?

I spent the rest of the week watching my workmates, observing how, and more importantly, why they did things. As a matter of course, they all wore gloves, as did I. It was still cold, May and the puddles were frozen over, all day.

The nature of the work was hard on the hands too. The rock and dust were abrasive, creating little cuts and sores that exacerbated chilblains. The cold and poor blood circulation to the extremities slowed and sometimes prevented even simple cuts from healing.

Why were colleagues removing their gloves? I needed to find out. That was why I was watching. Observing the guys who had kept me safe when I arrived, as a tyro. I had lost count of the number of warning shouts, thumps on the shoulders accompanied by vigorous gesturing at some piece of machinery swinging my way.

I owed these guys. So that is why I was going to tell the safety guys what I had seen.

It was a bigger group than I had expected. The Safety Team weren't represented by my pal Knut. Oh, no. He was

33

sat next to the Head of Work Place Safety; I caught the name Dag, as he was introduced to me by a suit I had never met. The Head of Production, The Deputy Chief Engineer and a lady called Ana from Personnel.

I was offered a seat at the table and Knut explained why I was at the meeting. I was one of the Outside Men, I had an understanding of the issues that caused my colleagues to work without gloves.

As I say, I owed my colleagues, so I did my best to explain the way the guys were balancing risk. Slipping off their gloves to enable them to pick something up quickly, first time and regaining awareness of what was going on around them, versus fumbling head down trying to get a grip in gloves, eyes well and truly off the ball!

I tried to rationalise the hand placed on the bucket of a digger. By doing that you knew where it was while you were concentrating on another part of your job. A hundred and one little things that made life safer in the warmer months, things that could come back and take a finger, a hand, an arm or your life in the depths of winter.

"How do stop this from happening?" I was asked.

"We train them all in frost safety; what

more can we do?" Dag, the Head of Work Place Safety demanded.

At least nobody asked, "why are they so stupid?"

"How many notified 'safety-breach incidents' do we have in a year?" I knew of about four after I arrived.

One of which was indoors, when someone had grabbed a broken handle on an exterior door, his bare hand had made contact with metal that was continuous to the outside world. He suffered a minor frost burn and lost about a square centimetre of skin.

The rules were clear, gloves on before attempting to open an exterior door. People had been complaining of the cold seeping in. "Is the door properly shut, Bjørn?" The door was closed tight … but the heat was being sucked out along that metal bar.

"We have a dozen or so that cause a stoppage each year." That surprised me. "Yes, they nearly all happen between September and December."

"While the men are unlearning their summer behaviours," I mused.

"So it seems." The Senior Manager, so senior I had not been introduced by name, was doodling on his pad. I took it as a sign he was listening carefully. "We do refresher training in the fall every year, don't we?"

"Yes, Sir." The Training Lead reacted as if he had been accused of causing deaths. "Every August, every man! We cover the winter policies in detail and every man signs to say he has understood."

I could see a couple of problems that might exist, it wasn't my place to get involved. I didn't need to.

"So every August the men sit through a lecture they have all heard before and sign to say they were in the room when it happened."

"That's what the policy says, Sir."

"Any comments? Anybody?" His eyes swept around the table, settling on me.

Sheep, lambs and slaughter were the words in the forefront of my mind. "I suppose it ticks a box on the policy documents, it won't do much more." I glanced about the room, everybody appeared to be listening, listening to me.

"Continue, I see from your expression you have more to say young Mr Graduate Engineer."

The big bosses knew about me!

"As you correctly identified, there are a lot of men who have heard this all before. They don't just switch off, they get resentful of an 'Indoor Man' trying to 'teach Granny to suck eggs', as we say in Britain. A person with little or no experience trying to teach people who have done something and know how to do it. The men know about the danger and have lived with it for years!" I was on a roll. "I have thought of two things that might help; both will need a bit of soft engineering."

"So we have to spend lots to get beyond where we are now!" Dag, the Safety Man protested.

"A few thousand Krona and a bit of your teams' time." I tried to placate the man.

"Details?" The Big Boss interrupted a protest from the Safety Man.

"No. Not yet. They are just ideas, I need to mull them over, to analyse the strengths and weaknesses. Every idea is like a two-edged sword, I need to make sure the side we apply is the sharper!"

"How long?"

"I have a trip booked next week, then it will depend on how much time I have free."

"You will have a week, full time, full pay and a desk in one of our offices. Three weeks today, same time, same place, Gentlemen." He gathered his pens and notepad and swept out of the room.

June 1975

"Nice is nice," I decide, as I wander along the Promenade des Anglais, on the sea front in Nice.. The sun is warm, even dressed in a t-shirt and a pair of shorts. The sun is climbing in the morning sun, glinting off the small waves that reflect the blue of the sky. I can't help but remark how different it looks to the grey-green of the stormy North Sea.

"This is what I want, maybe not today, but what I want. This is why I am freezing my assets off in the Far North." I go in search of a cup of coffee for less than ten Francs, in a moment of madness I looked in an estate agent's window. "I still want this, not today and at those prices not here either!"

*****

There is another downside of Nice for the unwary visitor from the Land of the Midnight Sun. The sun! I didn't do anything daft, well that was what I thought when I left the Promenade. I had listened to Mum, on those long-ago holidays in Wales and Cornwall.

"Take it easy the first day," She'd say. "Don't spoil the holiday by getting burnt on the first day!"

"I did, Mum honest!" I had kept my t-shirt on, all the time! After the cup of coffee, I had wandered into the old town, window shopping until lunchtime. A bowl of *moules avec frites* in a nice little pavement restaurant washed down with a small jug of white wine. I'd taken my cue from other dinners! Then a long pause to digest before ordering a *mousse au chocolat.* I finished with another one of those tiny coffees while I sat and watched the world go by.

I had carefully avoided sitting in the sun; so why was I bright red from elbow to wrist and mid-thigh to my socks. I looked like a bar of strawberry and cream nougat.

I ran a cold bath. OK, I ran a cool bath and lowered myself into the cold, well it felt very cold, water. I wallowed for as long as I could, allowing the heat to be drawn out of my burnt skin.

"What," I wondered, as I coated my glowing limbs with after sun, "would have happened if I had gone in for a swim?"

The bottle of suntan lotion on the bathroom shelf caught my eye. "Yes, Mum, before I go out tomorrow."

*****

It was forty degrees outside again, except it was Fahrenheit, not the centigrade it had been in Nice. The trip had clarified my goals. I wanted to be able to spend my life on the shores of the Mediterranean Sea, basking in a warm, blue sea. Eating in the great outdoors. The holiday I had planned to have at the end of my time in the darkness of the Norwegian winter had become the stepping board for something more. I wasn't sure what yet, but I had months to fill in the details.

Except Mr Sod had other plans for me and invoked his Law again.

Knut led me into the Big Bosses meeting, then left me in the room, alone. Apart from the Boss himself, a couple of other suits, from Head Office in Oslo and Ana from Personnel. There were no signs of Dag or the Training Manager. This meeting was shaping up to be slightly different from the last one.

"This is our British Graduate Mining Engineer. He has some ideas about how we make the mine safer as the winter comes on. Go on young man, wow us!"

So I did my best. I talk about my colleagues being intelligent men. Doing what they think is the best they can to keep themselves and their workmates safe.

"One of the things they lack is

information," I am getting into my stride. "The people in the offices here get the weather forecasts and can look at the thermometers. Mid-shift the men outside have no idea if it is cold, very cold or killing cold. I suggest we adapt the beach warning flags and put up a light system, different colours for the temperature band and update the status hourly."

That opened up a conversation that ran for an hour before I put the standby version on the table; flags with spotlights shining on them. Much easier to implement, cheaper and just as effective.

That was when they offered me the job.

By the end of the week, I was the Mines' Safety Engineer. My job was no longer to be a wielder of a pick and shovel in the killing cold of the Arctic winter. Now my job was to design and build cost-effective systems to stop the cold killing the people wielding picks and shovels, driving machines or just popping out to have a look at the situation. So much easier? No! Then, when I went into mining engineering it was never going to be as safe as one designing the new door handle for the Morris Marina.

I did have a substantial pay rise. A monthly salary going into my Credit Suisse account. A bit less holiday than had been taking, but it was paid holiday and I could take a longer break. I would have to attend monthly meetings in Oslo. That had the upside of having the company pay for the first leg of my travel, if I timed my trips correctly.

The next three months were spent in getting red 'No Touch' lines painted on the machines, on to which thick, green, hand-shaped, plastic stickers were fixed in locations where touching was not considered a disciplinary offence. The insulating properties of the plastic would allow a frost burnt hand to be detached from the machine by the owner, with less damage. Not that we told my former brothers of the spade the full story.

"It is a disciplinary offence to touch the red! A repeated breach will be a dismissal offence. However, it is recognised there are times when you need physical contact for safety considerations. While the green temperature flag is flying, and only when the green flag is flying, you may rest an ungloved hand in the green areas."

I repeated the lecture time and time again. The Grunts listened, it was a new message, I had been with them in the Dark, I was still one of them. I was still outside for whole shifts several times a week. I would talk to them about their difficulties and worries.

It was suggestions from the mine face

that got the klaxon sounded every time the temperature flag changed. One day, in mid-September, the green flag was not hoisted, the winter had arrived.

I flew to England for a week at the end of that first month of winter. I missed seeing James, he was in Northern Ireland. Dec and I went out on the lash if you can call it that.

We met in the same pub as last time; I had longed for a pint of dark, malty, English beer ever since I had decided to head home. Dec had a half of some pale imitation of a continental beer, an almost alcohol-free pale imitation at that!

"I'm getting married on Christmas Eve." I almost fell off my stool.

"You are what?"

"I'm marrying Mary on Christmas Eve," Dec repeated.

Punch lines about arriving at the Church on a donkey or not so immaculate conception; fought to escape my mouth. Instead, I managed to utter, "You won't forget your anniversary in a hurry!"

"Something like that," he mumbled into his glass of gnat's piss.

"What prompted this sudden change of lifestyle?" I asked, suppressing the questions about shotguns and due dates.

"Tax relief; we were going to wait until the spring, then Mary's Dad pointed out that by getting married before April got me an extra year's Married Man's Allowance and the Mortgage Interest relief on the new house." Dec was trying to act grown-up; I could still sense the 'lad' trying to get out though.

"You old romantic you! This calls for another drink!"

"I'll just have another of these." He pointed at his glass. "Then we can move on to the curry house."

I had misjudged how serious he was. At the bar, I resisted the strong temptation to get a scotch, or even a double, added to the lager.

We drank up and moved to the curry house. We barely glanced at the menu before ordering our traditional choices. Then it sort of went quiet for a moment or two.

"Tell me about Mary. How come we have never met her?"

"She was my girlfriend forever, back before I went to Uni." Now that I didn't know. "We had a big fight over me going out with other girls while I was away."

"I can imagine!" I smiled. We had, perhaps surprisingly, been a fairly celibate bunch, despite the reputation students had.

"No, you can't. I was promising to be faithful, to go home every other weekend to keep 'us' going. She was encouraging me to shag everything in sight and have fun!"

"Wow!"

"Yes, wow. That is what caused the row that led to her announcing that she was chucking me."

"Shit"

"Then when I got back home, I held a door open to let a woman in a wheelchair get into the shopping centre. I didn't realise it was her, until she had got through it. She had pretended not to recognise me."

"Bummer." At this point I was starting to wonder what had happened to my ability to construct sentences. "Why was she in a wheelchair?"

"Motor Neurone Disease."

"Oh!" This was bad, why had I not known any of this? Why hadn't Dec told me before?

"They had just diagnosed her when I was doing my 'A' Levels. She decided not to tell me about it. I was supposed to go to University and forget her." I waved the approaching waiter away. Dec needed space. "They think she has another five, maybe ten, years. I want to spend as much time with her as possible. So we are getting married on a special day as soon as we can."

"If there is anything I can do…" I couldn't think of anything beyond the platitudes you heard older relatives say at times like that.

"Actually, there is." Dec paused

'Oh, God! What is he going to ask?' I remember my hands starting to shake as Dec took a deep breath.

"Will you stand as my Best Man?" I admit I cried.

December 1975

The blue flag had been flying continually for two weeks. The temperature hadn't risen above minus eighteen in all that time. We had done really well, no serious incidents.

We had sacked two men for breaching safety rules. The surprising thing was, that on both occasions, the Unions had backed our decision. The safety of their members was more important than any individual's bad behaviour.

We introduced one more safety aid. An idea from one of the Outside Team.

He had come up to me late one afternoon in October. It was already dark, it looked like he had a piece of rope he wanted to show me. I'd pointed to an area with better lighting and where it would be a little quieter.

It was a piece of rope, one end tied around his wrist. On the other end, he had a magnet. He put his spade on the ground and dropped the magnet on to it … with the spade back in his grip, he pulled the magnet free and tucked it back into a pocket sewn onto his sleeve.

Blindingly simple, it meant he wasn't fumbling around on the ground trying to get his gloved hands around the dropped implement. It needed work but the extendable, plastic rod mag-grab is that magnet on a bit of rope. The chap who invented it is getting paid a royalty for his idea.

I had the two weeks into Christmas off; I would be back to supervise the small crew, charged with making sure nothing froze solid, between Christmas and the New Year.

Sunshine, warmth and a few drinks were the priority for the first week. Someone suggested I could hire one of the Director's apartment on the Canary Island of Tenerife, so I did. The place was fantastic, on the second floor with a balcony looking out to the south across the sea. It confirmed my dream. I wanted a place like this, maybe not with four bedrooms but a nice place in the warm sunshine. A place I could share, somewhere Mum and Dad could borrow. A place I could bring a girlfriend and eventually, who knows, children.

I had spent the day alternating between the beach and a bar with my book. 'See, I did listen, Mum, and I learnt from my mistake in Nice.' I showered, grabbed a beer from the fridge and went out on to the balcony. I sat there in the hazy late afternoon sun trying to work out how much longer I would have to work in the freezing hell I had left behind before I had saved enough.

I had reached the depressing figure of another four years. With that figure in mind, I decided that I might as well get dressed and head out for something to eat. Then I would look for a bar with some music or something and while away the rest of the evening.

I cheered up over my steak and chips. I realised that I had been saving far more slowly in the first months. Since then, my wages had gone up and, thanks to the paid travel to and from Oslo, my costs had gone down. For goodness sake, I wasn't even paying as much for the apartment as for my hotels in Paris and Nice. It might only be three years.

During a break from the music, (the guy on the keyboards was good, the girl singer had a nice voice; just she didn't understand the words. Her emphasis was on the wrong part of the lines. It was messing with my enjoyment of the songs, SilENCE is gOLden, gOLden, it just sounded wrong!) I caught a conversation at the bar.

A customer, a German, was trying to do a deal to pay his bill in deutsche marks, he and the bar owner were arguing over the exchange rate. The figures I was hearing suggested that he was going to be getting a much better rate in the bar than the banks were offering. Something must have happened to the value of the peseta or the value of the deutsche mark was soaring. I would need to keep an eye on the exchange rates, I might be able to shorten the time in the North to just a couple of winters!

*****

I arrived back in London Airport feeling much healthier than I had as I transited through on my way out to the Canaries.

Just as well, I had a stag night to organise. I got on the phone as soon as I arrived at my parents' house. It was then that I realised just how lonely Dec must have been, I had already received confirmation from James and Andreas to say that they were coming. Two of his school mates and another of the guys from Uni said 'yes'. "The works' Christmas Party" or "money is too tight at this time of year," was cited by a lot of people.

Still, we had a good night out and Dec had more than enough to drink, got curry down his front and was kissed by every member of a hen party we crossed paths with. The party had been suddenly enlarged by four deep-sea men. Two of the trawlers from Dec's fleet got into port that same day. I'm not sure if they were mates of Dec or had just latched on to a party offering a night on the beer; mates or not, they knew how to party.

*****

Mary turned out to be a delightful young woman. I almost forgot she was facing an early death sentence when she turned on her wicked sense of humour. I was happy and sad for Dec in equal measures. He had found someone who cared for him, someone who he cared for and they were going to be forced apart.

I kept my Best Man's speech short and honest. I really didn't want to say anything that might have put a damper on what was a very special day for my friend and his wife. Then, I would have had to embellish beyond recognition to get anything that would have made it on to a saucy postcard.

It was a small but happy wedding. It was great to see James and Lindsey again. I thought it very kind of Lindsey to come and find me after my speech. She wanted to say how pleasant it was to hear that we could be nice to each other.

Later, Andreas introduced me to Kate, 'why was this woman not a famous model?' And 'how come Andreas had held on to her?' Well, the second part was easy, if you liked tall, blonde-haired, ski instructor types with exotic accents. Visually they were a well-matched pair!

I managed a few words with the bride

before the happy couple left for their honeymoon. I asked where they were going.

"I know I'm not supposed to tell, in case you do something awful but seeing as it is you, we are going to a place in Menorca."

"That's a long way!" I was aware it was near Majorca and somewhere off the Spanish Coast.

"Yes, but I fell in love with it when I went there with Mum and Dad. I was fourteen and had never visited anywhere so beautiful. I know it won't be the same in December but I want to share it with Dec." The 'I don't know if I will ever be well enough to make the trip after this.' hung silently between us.

"Carpe diem, seize the day, make sunny memories for the darker days!" I squeezed her hand and fled with tears in my eyes.

Soon after the cake had been cut, Dec and Mary headed off for the airport and the Mediterranean.

I went and said goodbye to both sets of parents, thanking them for allowing me to be part of such a special occasion. More tears, this time as the mothers comforted each other.

I said a quick goodbye to Andreas. "See you in the office in a couple of weeks!"

Then I got a kiss from Lindsey and a hug from James as I reaffirmed of my promise to be there in June, for their big day.

"Take care, and remember, incoming has right of way!" Were my parting words to James. He had nodded. Then I was on my way south for Christmas Day with my parents.

March 1976

Things had been going well in the darkness, we hadn't lost a single shift's production. I was surprised that nothing had gone wrong, where was Mr. Sod? Then the call came, meeting, Monday, Oslo office, pack for a week.

It was that last bit that had me worried. Normally these meetings were overnight stays, why was I wanted for a week? Time would tell. I went to find my Shift Teams; they would need to be on the ball while I was away. I nearly bumped into Andreas as I was hunting for my outdoor boots.

"Going anywhere special?" He asked.

"Just out to find the Shift Safety Team," I replied.

"Oh?" He carried on with his mission. I had heard a question mark; I am sure he was expecting a different answer.

*****

I was sat on the plane South, I couldn't find my book, I'd left it somewhere and that got me thinking. From there I found myself thinking about Andreas.

'Come to Norway, I'll get you a job' and there was a job for me. 'Indoor job', "Andreas is working for you." Andreas had known something about this meeting I was going to.

"Who is Andreas?" I resolved to find out.

*****

Monday, the mystery deepens. I am invited into an office to meet a couple of men I have never seen before. Men in bespoke suits wearing expensive shoes with Rolex watches adorning their wrists. I felt very scruffy in the business jacket and tie I had bought after my first appearance at an Oslo Meeting. Maybe I should have got a haircut and a proper shave on the way to the office.

'Pointless!' I chastised myself for thinking I could get into the game. 'They dress to impress all the time. They would turn up in flash ski-gear with a designer parker over the top if they had to come North.'

There was a reason I had never seen them before, they were lawyers. American corporate lawyers: they had something they called a 'Confidentiality Agreement' for me to sign.

"So what is all this about?" I gestured to the inch-thick wad of papers in front of me.

"We are really glad you asked that, son."

'Sarcasm, the lowest form of wit', I was wrong. They were Americans, they meant it.

"It makes it so much easier to explain if you want to hear what we have to say." Lawyer Two expanded on his colleague's answer. I recognised the sentiment, my, 'Let's be careful out there' lectures always went better with an interested audience. They got their nickname from the phrase I had stolen from the TV series 'Hill Street Blues.' The Sergeant leading the morning parade used to conclude by pausing and saying, "Hey … Let's be careful out there!"

Now when I did a briefing I'd do the 'Hey' and the guys would chime back, 'Let's be careful out there.' From how that phrase came back I could gauge how attentive they had been. A couple of times I had felt it necessary to call the group back and check they had understood the message. "What are you going to do different today to be safe … Jan?" Pose, pause and pounce; I read that in a book about giving a briefing.

Back in the office, the two legal eagles explained, "You are going to hear a lot of stuff, much of it way above your pay grade, over the next few days. In the event that any of it emerges anywhere else, this pile of papers gives us the right to sue you for everything you own."

59

"Right down to selling all your organs and the chemicals the rest of your body is made from." Lawyer Two reinforced what his colleague was implying.

"That's only if we find that you have been talking about any of it to anybody who has not signed these papers." The friendly, less threatening, Lawyer One explained.

They had done a good job of explaining the scope and remedies laid out in this agreement.

"How do I know who has signed these papers?" It seemed a fair question to ask.

"You don't and if anyone says they have … you tell us. Clause 17."

"That is the one that says, 'communicating the existence of *the Agreement* is of itself a breach of *the Agreement* and will invoke the remedies listed at Annex 23.' It makes it simple, say nothing to nobody, except in the meetings you are invited to attend." Lawyer Two seemed to get all the good lines.

"If I don't sign? Just for instance of course." I had picked up the pen, a Mont Blanc, of course, to signal my intention to sign.

"Is it as dangerous, up there in the

North, as they tell me?" Lawyer One being sarcastic?

"It must be this guy knows how to live dangerously!" Lawyer Two's response encourages me to sign on the dotted line and the bottom of every page. It was just as well I wasn't signing in blood! Although, I did get a coffee delivered at about page one hundred.

Whatever was happening was very serious. I was given a sealed envelope and told to read and remember the information.

"Tuesday, 08:45. Report to the Reception Desk. Identify yourself, your Corporate ID Card would be best. Declare that you have a meeting with 'Direktør Pedersen.'
You will be collected by someone who will ask if you 'are here to see Sigurd.'
You will reply 'I thought it was Thomas.'
You will follow your escort, in silence."

After I had read it, the piece of paper was taken from my hands. I watched as it was torn into small pieces. Some of the bits went out of the window, some into Lawyer One's pocket and rest into the bin.

This was, as some of the guys at Uni would have said, 'Heavy shit, man!'

*****

Seeing as it has all happened. The Stock Markets have absorbed the changes. All the people involved, winners and losers, know their fates. The newspapers have reported the outcomes and discussed the potential futures ad nauseam.

I kept quiet. Spoke only when asked a question. In the end, I got a promotion and sent away on a week's leave to get over all the excitement.

I admit I was buzzing and anybody who knew me would know something was up. The corporate people fixed up the arrangements.

"Where do you want to go?" A good question, I had nothing planned. Then I remembered my conversation with Mary.

"What is Menorca like at this time of year?" It sounded a lot better than anything the Arctic Circle had to offer. The Corporate Travel woman booked me flights, a hotel and a car. Along with the tickets she handed me an envelope "for out- of-pocket expenses, a change of clothing and things like that."

When I was in the taxi to the airport, I opened the package and found some Spanish banknotes, one thousand five hundred pesetas. What was the exchange rate back before Christmas, I racked my mind and kept coming back to one hundred and forty to the pound.

"A hundred pounds!" The taxi driver gave me a funny look in the mirror. I was babbling in English. I was rich for the week. A British tourist was only allowed to take fifty pounds out of the country, no matter how long they were going for.

The hotel was miles away from the airport, still, I did get to see the whole island. It was however worth the drive. The former capital of the island Ciutadella immediately captured my imagination. Narrow, crowded streets, a tiny working harbour and the spectacular orange cathedral. The temperature was pretty good too, not too hot.

The hotel was fabulous; according to the information pack, it was a converted hostel for the nuns and pilgrims. I doubt they would have enjoyed the luxury of a double bed to themselves, for most of their stay, and a private bathroom.

There were plenty of restaurants and bars to visit; after a couple of days, it was time to explore. I started by driving back to Mahon at the other end of the island, another interesting harbour town. On the way back, I stopped to pick up a hitcher, she turned out to be Dutch but she spoke really good English. I teased her a bit by slipping into Norwegian from time to time, which made her laugh.

"Why are you on Menorca at this time of year?" She asked.

I explained about my job in Norway and needing to get some sun without getting too hot.

"Cool." She wriggled into a more comfortable position. "It is a nice island, isn't it?"

"Yes it is, just a bit less … I don't know. My friend had built up my expectations and it isn't quite doing it for me."

"Where have you visited?"

I told her, about the two cities.

"No wonder, you need to take the side roads, like that one!" She pointed to a narrow turning off the main road.

"Not this evening, tomorrow. I need to get something to eat."

"Fine, I will show you some of the places tomorrow." She laughed and stretched.

We had a paella at a place away from the centre of the city. A few houses and a bar overlooking a tiny beach, with some rowing boats pulled up on the sand. This was what I had been expecting from the island.

Over dinner and a couple of local beers, I discovered that Janna worked on a yacht that sailed out of Mahon. One of a crew of four that did the sailing, the cooking, the cleaning, and waited on the rich clients that chartered the yacht for two or three weeks at a time.

"It sounds pretty idyllic," I foolishly commented.

"When the clients are off the boat, it isn't so bad. The rest of the time we are trying to run the boat and stay out of sight. Pretending you don't hear the drunken arguments. Ignoring the sexual advances of the men and sometimes the wives too. Cleaning up after them. Nah, it is far from perfect but it pays."

*****

The following day we explored, I explored, Jenna guided me, down some of the side roads. At the end of some were villages like the one we had eaten in the night before. Others ended in larger 'urbanizations', villages being built around larger bays for tourists. Some tracks ended. Just stopped in the middle of nowhere. A small beach, a few dunes and the sea.

It was on one of these beaches we made love. A first for me, I was pretty certain Jenna had indulged before. I was stunned, as she announced she was going to clean herself

65

up and walked, naked, to the sea, rinsing herself.

By the time she returned, I was ready again. This time we both walked naked to the water. another first for me.

"We don't do that sort of thing on the beach normally!" Jenna informed me as I steered around the potholes in the track.

"We?"

"FKK people; normally we just swim, sunbathe and relax. Today, there were no families and I like you."

"You'll have to explain FKK to me."

"I will, over dinner."

"Dinner?" I looked at the clock on the dashboard, it was later than I believed possible. "Where do you suggest?"

Another Cala: I'd discovered that 'Cala' meant inlet. A bar with a man barbequing fish and meat, which would be served with bread, salad and boiled potatoes. I'm not sure if he was a great cook or it was the ambience... when I think back, I can still taste that dorada.

*****

The next day we repeated the whole thing, different roads with similar endings.

"Dinner?" I did the asking this time.

"It will have to be by the harbour."

"Oh?" I was surprised by the imperative, in everything else we had just gone with the flow.

"Yes, my ferry is tonight."

"Ferry?"

"Yes, I have to leave, I re-join the yacht tomorrow. The boatyard should have completed the refit."

That was a bit of a bugger, I had another whole day before I had to catch my flight. Jenna must have seen something in the look on my face.

"Ask the hotel for a map showing how to get to Cala Macarella; it is a bit of a walk, but well worth it. If you are feeling energetic, you can cross over the headland to the smaller bay, Cala Macarelleta. I love it when we get to moor up there."

That was it, I had a plan for the next day. We went back to the hotel, had a quicky, collected Janna's bag and headed out. A few beers and a steak and I walked Janna to the ferry, which blazed with lights in the small harbour.

"That was fun, I'm glad to have met you. Keep safe in your frozen wilderness!"

"And you be careful on the storm-tossed seas!" I replied. "And, Janna, thanks for showing me around."

I wandered back to the hotel alone. Asked for the map and the receptionist marked the route for me.

*****

Cala Macarelleta was well worth the scramble through the wooded headland. The cliffs on both sides trapped the sunlight, it was pleasantly warm. There was only one couple, enjoying the sun a hundred metres or so distant, closer to the water.

I sat and tried to make sense of the previous week. The secret meetings. The interrogation about the safety record at the mine. The plotting and discussions taking place in rooms I was barred from entering.

In the end, the 'merger', as the friendly takeover was going to be announced to the press, was all agreed. The American Mining giant was going to get a foothold in Europe.

The Directors of the struggling Norwegian firm would get a good price for their shares. The mine would get some fresh investment. I had a new job. Based at the mine, but with Europe in my title. The Americans have big plans for moving forward.

I am suddenly aware that my legs are burning in my jeans. Perhaps, I should move. Then I hear a shriek, I look to where the couple were splashing in the shallows, splashing naked. FKK, Janna had explained it.

"Why not?" No one who I would ever see again would see me. I stripped off my jeans, underwear and shirt followed. I spread myself out, face down on the sand.

I must have dozed off; I hadn't slept much over the past few days. When I woke up there more people on the beach.

Children! I could hear children.

"FKK is for families. That is why we don't normally do this, except on an empty beach." Janna's voice sounded in my head. I rolled over slowly.

Three more couples and a family had arrived. One of the women was in a bikini. The mother of the family was topless and everybody else was bare. Including the two children trying, with limited success, to bat a ball to and fro.

I watched for a few minutes. To all intents and purposes, it was like watching people on Bournemouth beach on a Tuesday afternoon. Why were they naked when they might as well wear a costume?

Time to move, I pulled on my underpants, then stood to get dressed. I must have put on weight; my trousers felt tight on my legs. My shirt had shrunk too, it was catching under my arms and felt tight across my shoulders.

That made no sense, so I put it out of my mind and set off to where the car was parked. The scramble over the headland had been fairly light work on the way to the beach, now, it was a sweaty struggle. I was soaked by the time I got back to the car.

June 1976

It had been a real bugger the past couple of months. The Merger went through. A ream of American 'Consultants' arrived. They held meetings with the miners. Then they held one to one interviews with some of them. At that stage, the people who knew most about what the American 'USMM Corp' was doing were, surprisingly, the Union Officials. Someone had explained the power of the Unions in most Scandinavian countries. They were involved, engaged and there was no sign of unrest.

The next phase revealed what had been going on. The Managers, starting pretty near the top were called for, one at a time, for face-to-face meetings. Few ever appeared again, vanishing into thin air. The few that did return to their offices remained tight-lipped, then they too disappeared a few days later.

*****

"They offered to accept severance without arguing. The others, the ones that wanted to argue were shown their disciplinary dossier and resigned or were sacked." Andreas explained this after the Consultants had left.

"How do you know all about these

things, Andreas?" I asked. I still hadn't worked out how come he had made those enigmatic statements that came true. "It isn't as if you were in Oslo for the meetings."

We were interrupted by the Mine Manager joining us. It was the first meeting of the new slim-line Management Team. Me, Andreas, Kristiana from staffing and Mr. Haugen, the only remaining member of the old Management Team.

"Welcome all." Mr. Haugen opened the meeting. "I suppose we should start as you will have to continue, Mr. Pedersen." He gestured towards Andreas.

"Thank you, Mr. Haugen, I shall be relying on your support over these next months."

'Andreas? Andreas Peterson? Andreas Pedersen? Had I misheard his name in that pub those months, years, ago?' The tumblers began to fall into place.

'Direktør Pedersen', Andreas knowing all about *things*, almost before they were announced. 'Andreas is working for you.' Andreas Sigurdsen as he would have been under the old Patronymic naming convention.

The meeting was suitably short. Keep on keeping on, was the message. The new owners wanted to keep the operation profitable. They did not want to drive increased profit or turnover. The goal was to prove that they were careful owners. That they could be trusted to run mineral extraction facilities that matched, or outperformed, the best in Europe. They wanted to be partners of choice for intervening in failing mines. White, not black, knights from the point of view of Governments and Unions.

I could tell that Mr. Haugen knew about Andreas. I worked out that Kristiana would have known something from the Personnel Records, that were now part of her domain, as was housing and feeding the workers.

As I was the only one in the dark, I collared Mr. Pedersen after the meeting.

"Andreas, I think I need…" That was as far as I got.

"I've known today was coming since … well, since forever. That is why I put up with Dad's start at the bottom bull! I worked outside for a year before I got a Team Leader's job. Then I was moved into the office as a gofer, you know go for this, go for that. Then I became the Management Trainee two years ago." He paused, to see if I had grasped the significance.

"Then you started to visit England?"

"No, I'd been doing that while I was outside, cheap beer, remember?" He laughed. "I met you, an unemployed mining engineer. Someone about my age, a guy I got on well with. A potential right-hand man, an ally, so I pulled strings."

"The job? The promotion? The mission to Oslo?"

"The job, I opened the door, you moved in and made yourself at home. The promotion? I was just the Management Trainee. OK, Personnel might have known about my family, but all I could do was throw your name into the conversation. You proved yourself to the Management. Then you got the results that made the Americans demand to meet you, to see if you were genuine."

I must have looked doubtful.

"You are here because you are good at what you do. I am here because I am my father's son and I showed good judgement in bringing you into the organisation. You are proven, I'm on trial!"

*****

Outside, in the nearly endless light, the guys continued to extract ore from the ground without getting themselves killed or injured. In the office, we concentrated on making sure the coffee and fuel arrived before stocks had run out, the men got their holiday, their pay and all the movies they could watch.

*****

The wedding of Miss Lindsey Anne Margaret Holstein-Hall to Captain James Alexander Hesketh-Stuart was a posh event. I had invested in a new, bespoke suit as soon as I got home. If I was going to many more meetings with the American owners' European team, I needed some 'special schmutter' and I was going to look as if I belonged. I had chosen to give it a first outing at my friend's wedding.

It turned out to be a good job I did. On two levels.

The first was, it was a very upmarket do, the jewellery on display was a match for the display in the Tower of London. At least as I remembered the Queen's Collection from a school trip over fifteen years earlier.

There were a lot of men and a few women in their best uniforms, the families in morning suits and silk dresses. The bride and the bridesmaids were in traditional, white, meringue confections. They looked stunning, one of the bridesmaids in particular.

To be honest, even in my new suit, Dec,

75

Mary and I looked like the charity cases we were. It didn't seem to matter to the other guests, "Old money, not like the *nouveau riche*," Dec suggested.

He might have had something.

During the Wedding Breakfast, (more of a late lunch but that was what it was called on the invitation) I was seated next to Henry, Lord Rochester. He was miserying to anyone who would listen, about how impossible it was proving to buy a '*pied a terre*' in the Dordogne.

"The place is going for a song. I have the money sitting in the bank. Everything set and the damn Government won't let me spend my money."

I had, of course, heard about the Exchange Control Regulations. Rules introduced to stop people exporting money, something to do with the balance of payments.

"Even if I gave the entire household staff the fifty pounds to take out, we would have to go three times to move enough money to France," His Lordship continued.

"You must have a large household, based on the price of places in Nice!" I joined in the conversation.

"Good Lord, some of those places on

the Riviera! I would need to move the maximum every day for a year. No, Old Chap, this is a rural retreat. A farmhouse and a few acres of vines. A gathering place for the Grand-children is the idea. It needs a bit of fixing up but we can do that bit by bit until the restrictions are lifted."

"Not a problem I face," I reply. Then I see the look on his face. "My money is all in Swiss Francs." I tuck into my dessert. A few minutes later, His Lordship puts his cutlery down and turns to me properly.

"You were saying, you have money in an account in Switzerland?"

"Yes, I manage a mine in Norway, I decided to be paid in a stable currency."

"I don't suppose you have ten thousand pounds in some foreign currency I could buy off you?"

"How do you mean, My Lord?"

"Call me Henry. Look, I have to find something over fifty thousand in French Francs for the purchase and some extra for the immediate renovations. If you can see a way of transferring that sort of sum to my French bank account, I would make it worth your while. Very worth your while." He took a sip of his wine. The speeches were about to start.

"I don't think this is the right time for this conversation. Can I give you a call on Monday, Henry? I think we might be able to do business." I took his card and ostentatiously placed it safely in my wallet. "After lunch, Monday then."

The speeches were typical wedding speeches. I knew half the things that were said about James by the Best Man were, to put it nicely, distortions of the truth. Still, I laughed along and enjoyed the entertainment.

There was a pause in proceedings while the tables were cleared and the band was getting set up. I found Dec fussing over Mary; she had overdone things slightly. Insisting on walking to be greeted by the Mother of The Bride and the couple. She was now sat in her chair looking a little pale.

"Leave me be Dec, I'll be fine in a minute or two, please love."

I asked if they had enjoyed the Breakfast and the speeches.

"Well, it sounded to me that Dec has not told me all the tales of your time in University!" Mary laughed, some of the colour came back into her cheeks.

We had been chatting for a few minutes, before James pushed through the well-wishers.

He exchanged pleasantries with Mary, pointed out a door to a quiet room if she needed a bit of space at any time. Then he turned to me.

"I have a favour to ask, one of my guys managed to get himself blown up slightly last month. He is still not confident on his injured leg, I wondered if you could escort one of the bridesmaids in his place?"

"What exactly would I be volunteering for?" I was concerned in case it was anything too complex, I didn't want to mess up something special.

"Just lead Lindsey and me onto the dancefloor for the First Dance and stand there looking pretty until it is time for the general shuffling to start."

That didn't sound too onerous, anything for a mate. "Of course, James. Lead on."

*****

"Delighted to meet you, Sophia!" I certainly was. Sophia was *that* special bridesmaid.

"Likewise, I'm sure." She smiled back. "I can tell from your voice you are not one of the noble class, are you one of James' army colleagues?"

"No, I'm just one of the guys who shared a house with him at Uni." I smiled back.

"A bit like me, I met Lindsey at college too." I could see her relax.

The formal bit of being part of the procession and standing around looking beautiful while James and Lindsey danced went well. Admittedly, Sophia was better at the 'looking pretty' part than me. I was just happy to have managed to walk properly.

We had 'shuffled around', as James had put it, for a couple of dances before I took a chance and let go of Sophia. "A drink, Sophia?"

"Yes please, and it is Soph. I hate the way the last bit of my name sounds. My Dad was such a fan of the actress, he was supposed to have registered my name Sophie Ann, instead, when he got back from the Registry Office, I was Sophia Lauren." The laugh in her voice told me she was relaxed, I felt some of the tension ease out of my shoulders.

There was only one slight problem, as Soph's escort, I suddenly went from being 'just a guest' to being a part of the event. Cutting the cake, we were there in the background of the pictures. Time for the Bride to get changed into her going away outfit. We were in the line-up as she retired from the reception room.

I was convinced Lindsey gave me a smile and a wink as she passed me.

The final set piece of the day, the departure for the honeymoon. Just before they headed off, James waved to me, I pushed through the melee surrounding them.

"I just wanted to say thank you for stepping into the breach and looking after Sophia all afternoon. Sadly, Clive had to leave early. He should have listened to the Medics and stayed in hospital."

I had just worked out that Clive must have been the chap caught by the IRA bomb, when Lindsey delivered a kiss on my cheek. "Look after Soph for me! You make a good couple!"

I hadn't taken that in either before they were off heading to the car. As the photographer set up his shot, I worked my way through the throng to be seen escorting the bridesmaid I had been charged with caring for. That was what I told people as I trod on their toes. I half recognised a face, then a burly chap stepped between us so I kept moving.

"Did I just see one of the Princes?" I asked Soph when I reached her, ranged up with all the bridesmaids and their Officers to see the couple off.

"Quite probably, Lindsey was one hundred and eighty-something in line to the throne when I first met her. There have been a lot of babies since, but she is related."

Before I could respond, a cheer went up and the photographer started dancing around. His flash going off dazzled me. I was aware of a sudden movement; I blinked my eyes in time to see Soph holding the bridal bouquet aloft. Then, she had her arms around me and her lips pressed fiercely against mine.

'Nice!' I thought, then the kiss softened, 'nicer still!'

"You're a sly one Sofa!" I noticed the deliberate mispronunciation. One of the other bridesmaids had decided to interrupt what was getting to be a very tender moment. "You didn't tell us about this one, when is the big day?"

Ah, yes, the woman who catches the bride's bouquet is supposed to be the next one to get married. We had only just met but what the hell!

"Next June, if all goes to plan!" I announce.

Things go crazy for a bit; I am reassured by the fact Soph hasn't let go of my hand. Then the band starts playing again and the crowd thins, suddenly it is just us.

"Thank you for covering for me, those girls have been flaunting engagement rings at me all week." Soph has her eyes on the floor. I knew what I wanted to say but the confidence to say it had ebbed away.

Soph continued, "I guess it was that and the netball instincts, something thrown into my area; I jump and catch it!"

"I'm glad you did!" I was interrupted by a cough from behind us.

"We are leaving, Mary is getting very tired." It was Declan, a huge grin on his face. I noticed that Mary was smiling at us, a look of satisfaction on her face.

"Soph, this Dec, Declan, and his lovely wife Mary. Dec and I used to share a house with James." I do the introductions.

"It is so nice to see this old reprobate looking so happy, Soph, you must both come to dinner sometime and tell me your secret." As Mary was talking, I realised I had a smile fixed to my face.

With that, Dec clapped me on the shoulder and wheeled Mary away.

*****

I had suggested that we slip off and find

somewhere quieter to get to know each other. Soph had agreed, I had called for a taxi while she went to get changed. I had left my car at my hotel; I wasn't going to risk driving.

The taxi on the way, Soph now changed into a smart outfit, we went to take leave of our hosts.

"You have got yourself a cracker there, son!" Lindsey's father glanced over to where Soph was taking her leave of our hostess. "I gather you know that though, I hope it all goes well next summer, I'm sure Lindsey will tell us all about it!"

"Thank you, Sir" What else could I have said?

"I also hear you are going to be doing some business with Henry, make sure you get a good price. He is rich enough to pay for what he wants!"

"I will, Sir" I feel Soph's presence by my side. "Thank you, both, for the wonderful day." There was a gentle tug on my arm and I turned away.

*****

The taxi had delivered us to the Royal George, the inn where Soph was staying. I thought that it sounded a better place to head for than the Post House where I had a room.

I was right, it was better than many a traditional inn too. The low, beamed ceilings, the large bar with several hand pumps and a wall full of spirits, stood along the far wall. It looked like the perfect place to enjoy a few pints. I ordered a pint of ale and the martini and lemonade that Soph craved.

"Why don't you take them through to the Guest Lounge, Sir? The Landlord suggested as he took the money. "Just ring if you need anything." He pointed to a bell push on the wall as he showed us into the room.

The Guest Lounge looked exactly like it sounded, chairs and settees grouped around a low table, in each of three corners of the room. We selected a group by the, fortunately unlit, fire place. I put the drinks on the table.

"You take the sof... settee, I'll sit here." I had just caught myself in time. "Sorry, I now understand why you dislike being known as Sophia."

"Thank you, for noticing, now come and sit on the sofa next to Sophia." She fluttered her eyelashes at me.

*****

"I have never been outside of Oslo

85

Airport," Soph had just confided, when the Landlord popped in to ask if we would want food, as the kitchen would be closing soon. I checked my watch, half-past-eight already.

We ordered fresh drinks and a round each of cheese and ham sandwiches, still fairly replete from our meal at the reception earlier.

I had discovered that Soph, after having trained as a nanny, had decided that she didn't like most of the potential employers. She had applied to all the airlines for a job as a stewardess and been taken on by ScotAir. She was now regularly in Oslo, Stockholm and Malmo as part of their short-haul scheduled team. When she mentioned Oslo, I had of course suggested meeting up.

"You work in where?"

"Finnmark, Northern Norway," I replied.

"Why?" A perfectly reasonable question for a rational person to have asked.

"Do you want a full answer or just a quick one, Soph?"

"I'm not that sort of girl!" I was confused, Soph was laughing. "The short answer will do; for now!"

I suddenly recognised the accidental

double entendre, I feel my face going red. "Sorry, I wasn't, I mean I didn't take, I ..." Sophia was curled up laughing as I tried to dig myself out of a hole.

I stopped digging, took a deep breath, and waited for her to stop giggling. While I was waiting, the sandwiches arrived. We started on the food, chunky bread slices with generous slices of filling. I was hungry. My plate was empty as Soph picked up her last sandwich.

"Do you want a bit?" All innocence, maybe. Still, it got me laughing.

"Yes, please!" I enthused.

"I told you I'm not that sort of girl!" We were both giggling and snorting like a pair of teenagers. I suppose it was lucky we had the lounge to ourselves. Eventually, we regained our composure.

"OK, that short answer you were going to give me, why are you working in Northern Norway?" I could see that Soph was struggling to keep a straight face.

"Money," I replied.

"That was a bit shorter than I'd hope for!" We were both still suffering from the hysterics.

"That was a cruel thing to say!" My eyes were watering as I fought the rising urge to laugh. "I thought you said you weren't that sort of girl!" I was gone. Soph was trying hard to choke back her guffaws.

"You can give me the full-length version tomorrow." She chortled.

I stopped laughing. Tomorrow? Tomorrow! Had this perfect example of an English woman just suggested that I would be allowed to see her again? As soon as tomorrow. I held my breath, waiting for her to correct herself. She had stopped laughing too.

"I mean, only if you would like to see me tomorrow: if you have other plans …"

"If I had other plans, I would cancel them. I can think of anything I'd rather do than spend the day with you!"

"Oh! … I have to check out by ten tomorrow morning, we could meet then."

I was relieved, I wasn't going to be spending the night. She wasn't that sort of girl. The thought had made me smile.

"That sounds a good plan, what would you like to do?" I hoped she wasn't going to suggest hang-gliding or potholing. I would have done it alright, but like going scuba diving, it might have hampered the conversation.

"There are some wonderful walks around Lindsey's family estate. I'll ask our host if we can have a packed lunch and we can picnic."

The idea of sharing a little bite, al fresco with Soph held great appeal. Just, "this isn't going to be a 'hiking boots and anoraks' expedition, is it? Because I haven't brought that type of gear!"

"I'm not that sort of girl!" We both started to giggle again. "I was thinking in terms of strolling through a flower meadow, then resting under a large oak tree to picnic."

"Then that is what we will do!"

*****

Me and my big mouth, that had been a big invitation to Mr Sod to invoke his law.

I was back at the George bang on the dot of ten. I had, in reality, been parked around the corner, waiting, for a quarter of an hour. Soph was ready and waiting, she had stashed her bags in the boot of her car. I began to hope she was as keen as me.

Playing the perfect gentlemen, I leapt out of the car to open the door for her. I was rewarded with a kiss.

Settled in our seats, both instinctively reaching for our seatbelts, our hands touching as we fumbled with the buckles. I must confess that I fumbled a bit longer than necessary. I was enjoying almost holding hands.

"Where to, my Lady?" I did my best Parker impression.

"Towards the estate, Parker." Soph had recognised the silly voice. As a poor imitation of Lady Penelope's chauffer in Thunderbirds.

"Yuss, my Lady."

"Drive properly!" A gentle slap lands on my arm and follows through to my leg. I stopped trying to drive as if I had wooden arms and started to drive carefully. I didn't want to displace her hand.

"Where are we going?" I asked as we followed the road towards the house where we first met.

"There is a summer house by the estate lake, there is a little track down to it we used to take the horses along. I'll tell you when we are getting close."

"Are we going to be OK there?"

"Of course, it is vanishingly rare that the family ever comes this far from the house. All the staff will be busy tidying up and moving things up at the house. Besides, Lindsey's Mum is a poppet and won't mind at all."

"As long as you are happy, Soph."

"I'm very happy!" She squeezed my thigh. "The gateway is coming up, just there!" She pointed and I slowed and turned into the narrow track. A few yards off the road was a gate. I stopped the car.

"I'll just be a minute." Soph unbuckled, climbed out of the car and moved into the woods. Then reappeared with a key in her hand, unlocked the gate and opened it, waving me forward. "Pull up a few yards further on, I'll lock the gate."

I did what I was told; seconds later, Soph is back in the car. "Drive on, slowly." Her hand is resting on my leg again.

I drive forward and a few minutes later, the line of trees thins and I can see a stone building just ahead.

"Stop the car here, no point in us attracting attention to our presence." I must have had a question mark printed on my face. Soph continued, "I want to spend the day with you. Rather than explaining who we are to an

91

undergardener, who has been sent to see whose car it is, so that we can get him out from underfoot!"

I gathered that Soph did not have a high opinion of undergardeners. The plus side was the reassuring comment about her wanting to spend the day with me!

We had gotten out of the car, Soph was carrying a bag that held our picnic, I reached out to take it from her. She responded by taking hold of my hand. The day was just getting better.

Soph had suggested we walked around the lake clockwise, "That way we are on the far side from the house as the sun sets. We are less likely to be interrupted if somebody decides they want a stroll after tidying up."

It made sense to me. Then I'd have been happy walking through a pig farm if that is where Soph wanted to go! We strolled along, holding hands, chatting about the wedding, the birds, the trees and anything that took our fancy.

Out in the lake, there was a splash, we both turned to look. The picnic bag hit my leg, with a resounding clunk.

"What is in the bag?" I asked, as I tried to decide, pretend to be hurt for sympathy? or pretend to be the injured warrior, struggling on despite his wounds?

"I'm not sure, shall we look?" Soph started to pull out the contents, handing them to me. Two packs wrapped in greaseproof paper, sandwiches I guessed, Two bags of crisps, peanuts and chocolate biscuits. Then there was another paper parcel, a piece of pie, I wondered, a couple of apples and two cans of cola. The last thing out was a bottle of water, that was the culprit.

We had put it all back in the bag, I'd been told off for suggesting that we could have a biscuit, "Elevensies?"

"I've only just had breakfast, I bet you went for the full English at your hotel too!"

We had walked on; I had wrested possession of the bag from Soph. It was quite heavy; I really should have been carrying it all the time. My mind drifted to lunchtime, I envisioned the two of us, under a large broadleaf tree, sharing sandwiches, lounging on a … on a what?

"We don't have a picnic blanket or anything!" I blurted out, horrified by the omission.

"No matter, we can sit on the grass."

"But your skirt?" She was wearing a smart denim skirt and a wide-sleeved, cheesecloth blouse, an almost transparent cheesecloth top!

"It will only be a little dust; it will brush off." We walked on towards the stand of trees Soph had pointed out as our picnic spot.

That was when Mr Sod intervened.

We had been walking in pleasant sunshine and not noticed the tall. cumulus cloud developing behind us. That was until a gust of wind brought the first drops slashing down. Within seconds we were soaked through, even as we dashed for the shelter of the trees.

"Where did all that rain come from I am wringing wet!" And looking very attractive, her blouse was completely transparent. Her lacy bra was not much better. I wasn't any drier.

"It looks quite localised. It should have passed in an hour!" I look at the horizon that is now clear of clouds. We could have lunch now; it will be dry to walk back.

"But look at me, I'm drenched."

"So, I can see!" Her arms fly across her chest. "This might sound a bit … you know, but I think we should get out of these things and hang them up to dry. It will stop us from getting chilled."

"You can but …"

"You are not that type of girl." I held up my hand to win a chance to finish. "I am not about to spoil something I think is special for a cheap thrill."

"Yeah?"

"Yes, I want there to another tomorrow for you and me, Sophia." For some reason, I felt it was important to use her proper name just then.

"OK, but no peeking."

"I don't need to peek and I promise no touching." I started to unbutton my shirt.

"What do you mean you don't need to peek?" Soph turned her back to me and asked over her shoulder.

"I've seen already, your top went completely see-through as soon as it got wet!"

Soph started to giggle. "Good! I thought for a second you were going to say you weren't interested."

She turns back towards me, holds her

arms out, and we kiss. I help her out of her skirt and hang her clothes up on branches in the shelter of the tree's canopy. Then I doff my trousers and hang them up too.

We kiss again, I feel the thrill of her skin pressed against me. "We can't do anything; I have stopped taking the pill."

I am surprised to find I am glad to hear it. "That is OK, with me."

"What?"

"I don't want to rush anything; I want us to take our time. I would like our first time to be more special than something to do waiting for the rain to stop." My mind flashes back to my brief fling, making out on the beach with Janna. No, I didn't want a repeat of that type of encounter.

"You are a bit of a romantic, aren't you?" I nod. "And if I had said take me now! What would you have done?"

I smiled and moved to …

"IF! I said if!"

I pick up the picnic bag. "I would have done whatever you asked. Sandwich?"

We sat under that oak tree and ate our

picnic. We talked about our lives and our backgrounds. We also kissed and cuddled until after the rain had stopped.

The storm may have passed but our clothes were still damp.

"Urgh! I hate the thought of putting that cold, wet thing back on!" Soph was holding out her blouse between her fingers by the collar.

"There is an alternative," I tentatively offered.

"Oh?"

"While I was on Menorca, back in the spring, I met up with this Dutch lady. We visited a few beaches and she explained that she enjoyed being FKK. I worked it out that she was a nudist." I could see a concerned expression gathering on Soph's face. "She explained that FKK was for families. It was just like being on an ordinary beach, except some people were not wearing clothes. There were children playing games, people sunbathing and swimming. I found that I was much more comfortable after swimming without the damp, clingy bits of cloth."

"And?"

"I was just thinking that we might be more comfortable and warmer not wearing wet clothes; sort of naked."

"Naked?" Soph's arms were clamped across her chest. "What if someone sees us?"

"You said they wouldn't, that was why we were walking around the lake in this direction."

"But … "Her blouse touched her leg and she winced.

"We'd be warmer and drier."

"But …" She gestured towards the trousers I was holding in front of me.

"If I couldn't control myself? I've had plenty of opportunities…"

"True," She bent down to pick up her still sodden denim skirt. "I certainly can't wear this!"

"Put it in the carrier bag, I'll see If I can find something dry in my case when we get back to the car." I took my underpants off and threw them in the bag too. "Might as well do this properly."

"Sheep!" Soph rolled down her knickers and added them to the bag. Having noticed my confusion, she added, "I might as well get hung for a sheep as for a lamb! Now do something to take my mind off this!"

"I promised to tell you the full-length version of why I am working in Norway." I held out my hand. I took hold of her's and we started to walk towards the car.

As we walked, I recounted my tale of woe; university, the greeting cards and my need to escape. I told her about the advice from James about setting targets. How I had decided that besides taking holidays in sunny places, I needed a reason not to spend all my money on 'cigarettes and whiskey and wild, wild, women!'

"Oh, dear, I'd better be on my best behaviour!" Soph interjected.

"I thought you weren't that type of girl!" We both laughed.

"So what are you doing with your money?"

"Saving it, I have a plan and it might be about to take a big step forward!"

"Ooh, a secret plan? Or can I share it?"

"It is very simple; I want to have a little place in the sun of my own. A place I can call home. A place I can share with my friends and family."

"That sounds like a nice dream."

99

"It is more than a dream; it is almost within my grasp."

"Can I visit you there?"

I pulled her close and kissed her, "I'll be hurt if you don't," I whispered.

*****

Back at the car, I rummaged through my suitcase and found a clean spare shirt, I handed it to Soph.

"That should cover all the important bits!" I continued to rummage looking for the shirt and jeans I had worn while driving up here on Friday.

"That is the horses safe!" I looked up, Soph is buttoning up my shirt.

"Pardon?"

"I'm covered up, so I won't have to worry about scaring the horses now."

"I hope you are joking, Soph! When I first saw you at the ceremony yesterday, I thought you looked wonderful and when James asked me to look after the belle of the ball, the most beautiful woman I have ever met. I thought all my birthdays had come at once." I paused; I was desperate for the next bit not to sound creepy. "Today, I have seen nothing to make me change that opinion."

"But …"

"No buts about it. You could turn up, ten years from now, wearing a boiler suit and high-heeled hobnailed army boots and I would still know you are the most beautiful woman in the room. I will always remember the Sophia I have seen today."

"You are just trying to talk me out of my knickers!" Soph tried to make a joke of it.

"I have already done that; I am just hoping for a repeat!" I took her in my arms and held her close.

"I will have to leave soon; I have an early flight tomorrow."

"Do you have time for tea or something first?" I didn't want the day to end.

"Dressed like this?" She stepped back. "I might just get away with it, but I can't 'Ye Olde Tea Room' serving you without a tie on."

"Ah!" I eventually find the clothes I was looking for.

*****

The pub was still shut when we got back to The George where Soph's car was parked. I had hoped that we could sneak her in to get changed in the ladies, while I tried to distract the Landlord.

"It looks like I am going to have to drive home like this."

"You could still fish something a little bit better out of your bag; a pair of pants and trousers of some sort," I suggested.

"Good idea!" She jumped out of the car, with the bag of her wet clothes and hurried across to a blue Mini Estate. She opened the back doors and threw the bag into the car and pulled a holdall round so that she could open it. A quick rummage and she had a few bits and pieces clutched in her arms.

"Hello, Love!" The Landlord had just emerged from around the corner of the building. "Ah, so you did get caught in that storm, we wondered. Come inside to get changed. Would you, and your young man, like something to eat and a hot drink? Sorry, no alcohol until opening time!"

"That's very kind of you, a cup of tea would be most welcome!" I had called across the carpark, allowing Soph a few seconds to gather her thoughts. "Maybe a few biscuits, if you have them?"

102

"Certainly! Let yourselves in, I'll go and get the kettle on." He opened the door and went inside.

I walked over to where Soph was standing, clutching bits of clothing.

"Have you got everything Soph? Underwear, top and jeans?" I could see the jeans.

"Yes, I think so. Do you think he saw anything?"

"I was watching, there was nothing to see. Well, nothing that might have, as you put it, 'scare the horses'!"

"Beast!"

"Come on, let's get you dressed and a hot cup of tea!" I led her across to the pub door.

"I heard you got soaked, do you need a hairdryer or anything?" I hadn't expected such kindness from the Landlady.

"Thank you, but my hair is dry, I'll have to wash it when I get home, but it was kind of you to offer." Soph turned and headed toward the ladies.

"Not in there dear, please. Go through to

103

the lounge, a much nicer place to dress. I'll knock before I bring in the tray."

"Thank you, again you are so kind."

"We were young once, Miss. Now go and get dressed. Your young man can wait here if you would prefer." Soph took her bundle of clothes and headed off towards the lounge.

"I know where you would rather be, Young Man. Just that I think she needs a little time to herself." She was right of course; I saw that as soon as she said it. "Go sit in the bar, I'll call you when I'm about to take the tea in."

"Thanks. I don't suppose you have a sheet of paper and a pen I could borrow?"

"There's a pen by the phone and I can let you have a few sheets off the note pad, no need to bring them back though!" She laughed, as she disappeared into the kitchen.

I grabbed the pen and note pad from the shelf near the phone. Sat in the bar I wrote down my address in Norway and at my parents. Then I added every phone number I could remember.

The Landlady appeared carrying a tray laden with a teapot, cups, saucers and cake, home-made cake. "Do you want to take this into the lounge?"

"How much do I owe you for this?" I pointed at the tray. "We normally do a tea with sandwiches and cakes for two pounds fifty a head, but I haven't done the sandwiches or cakes … "

"No, excellent value," I pulled a fiver out of my pocket and handed it to the protesting woman. "You have been so kind, I'm sure you'd rather have had your feet up in front of the TV before the evening rush."

She had smiled and nodded and pocketed the note. "No need to rush off, the bar will be open in about an hour, in any case!" As she turned away, I heard her humming what sounded like, 'The Arms of Mary', the recent hit for the Sutherland Brothers.

I picked up the tray and carried it into the lounge. "Our hostess is quite a romantic!" I put the tray down.

"I hope she hasn't stolen your heart away!" Soph was dressed, she had put on a bit of makeup and brushed her hair. She looked stunning.

"What time do you have to be off? We can stay as long as we want, or until closing time, whichever comes first.!"

"About half an hour ago, so another half hour won't hurt!"

"Sheep!" I smiled.

"Yes, sheep and a cuddle." She snuggled in close, as I poured the tea.

*****

"I wrote my phone number down for you." The tea had gone cold, but we were both trying to drink it.

"Not just the one either," Soph smiled, delved into her handbag, pulled out a pen and a small notebook and wrote a number on it. "It is a shared house, so be careful what you say on the ansa phone!"

July 1976

It had been an exciting few days since the wedding. The day after, I had phoned Lord Rochester, after a conversation with a switchboard operator and then his PA, I finally got through.

"Sorry about the bother, this is a private matter, so I hadn't told my office staff to expect your call."

"Not a problem, my Lord."

"It's Henry!" He took a breath. "Look I am in a bit of a bind; I have a contract to buy the place we were talking about at the wedding. I have the money to pay, just the deal is in French Francs and the Government won't let me have them. I am prepared to pay a handsome commission to someone who can deliver one hundred and twenty thousand French Francs, to my notaire's account by the end of next week."

I had done my sums, I had enough in the Swiss account. I had checked the exchange rates. What is more, I had nothing to lose if the deal fell through.

"I can do it, twenty thousand pounds." I

was holding my breath.

"I was hoping for something closer to fifteen."

"At this morning's rate, it was about that at Central Bank rates." I paused. "Allowing for the retail bank's cut, their commission and mine." I had learnt a lot from running an international account, and a certain amount more about playing hardball from the Americans.

"Ah, I see your point, is there any room for manoeuvre on this figure." Henry hesitated. "How about seventeen?"

"Eighteen."

"How about meeting halfway; seventeen and a half?"

That was my target, a quick twist for a little more. "Agreed, for the Swiss Francs, conversion to French Francs is at your expense."

"That sounds a reasonable plan, I'll need to check with the Notaire about accepting the Swiss currency. Meanwhile, please start making the arrangements. I'll send a contract."

I read off the fax number of the broker I had engaged for this purpose earlier that morning to manage my money.

I had turned sixty-two-thousand of my hard-earned Swiss Francs into Sterling and made an extra ten per cent. The broker had suggested that he could get an annual return of seven per cent, without risk. A look into the windows of the building societies explained just how easy that would be.

That evening, I was about to have a family supper with my parents, when the phone rang. My Mum answered it, Dad and I never get phone calls.

Wrong; Mum holds the phone out towards me, "A young lady, asking for you!" If you had ever wondered what smug looks like, having seen Mum's face, I could describe it for you.

"Hello,"

"Hi lover, it's me!"

"Soph!"

"I hope you weren't expecting anybody else."

"No, no of course not, I am just surprised to hear from you. I assumed you'd be working."

"I got in about ten minutes ago and was going to put the washing on. What do you want me to do with your underpants?"

"Ah! The bag of wet stuff!"

"Yes. I forgot all about it."

This was all very embarrassing; Mum was hovering listening to every word.

"I'll need to check my diary; I think we might be able to fix up a meeting if I can get down to Oslo."

"Mum still there?"

"Yes, I'll give you a call tomorrow."

"Remember what I said about the ansa phone and maybe not Oslo."

"I will do Soph."

"Goodnight, think of me wearing your pants in bed tonight!"

Oh! Did I ache for her! "Good night Soph."

The kisses made me blush.

"Anybody we should know about?"

"Not yet, Mum." She had seen, and

heard, enough to make it pointless to lie. "But I am hopeful." The vision of Soph clutching that bridal bouquet, smiling at me after that first kiss, drifted into my mind. "Very hopeful," I add as a whisper.

*****

"Things are moving, our American owners are up to something. They want me to block out most of August for meetings in London and Paris." Andreas welcomed me back to our Finnmark base.

"That will be nice for you, how are things between you and the beautiful Kate?"

"That, my friend, will become clearer after this month in the South. Will you be able to cope all by yourself?"

"I'll need a long weekend to build my reserves before you disappear."

I could feel Andreas' eyes trying to drill through to my inner thoughts. I chose not to reveal all, yet.

"I expect that will be possible." His eyes were still fixed on me.

Together we had looked at the calendar and agreed on dates for my extended weekend. I wanted to get on the phone to Soph

111

to try and make firm arrangements. Andreas was still trying to find out what was going on in my life.

"I can see why you'd want a bit of time off before four weeks on duty, but you have just had a week away. Did something happen at James' wedding?"

"Maybe, maybe not. I'll let you know as soon as I know." I was saved from further interrogation by the phone. Andreas answered it, exchanged a few phrases.

"The railways, it's about our shipment schedule, I'll have to take it at my desk."

I took the chance to escape and, all togged up against the cool weather, I went to chat to the Duty Safety Officer. When I got back, Andreas had left the building. The note on my desk informed me he had gone into town, an HR issue.

I took my chance and called Soph's number. I had mentally prepared a message for the ansa phone. I was thrown when someone picked the phone.

"Hi, this is Soph, who are you hoping to speak to?"

"Uh! Soph! How wonderful, I thought you'd be flying!"

"Captain No-pants! I should have been but the plane went 'technical' on us and we didn't have the hours to continue."

That made little sense to me, but I blundered on. "Can you get a stop-over" (I had picked up a little jargon from the movies.) "somewhere warm for a few days? I have a short break from the 28th to 1st August."

"I'm sure I can, better still I can probably get a jump seat on our new Menorca charter flight. We have a new arrangement with Baker's Holidays. There's a thought, I might even be able to get us a deal on some accommodation too!"

"That is great, I'm so pleased that you sound as keen on this as I am!"

"Don't doubt it, I have some news for you. I have found a pack of my pills that I had leftover when I stopped them, I'm going to start taking it next week."

"I… I … I …" I am stuck for words, I take a deep breath. "If you are sure, I'll start packing straight away!"

"Calm down, we'll have to wait a couple of weeks for them to work. Hmm, I make that about the 27th, convenient, what?"

"Just as well I can't reach you from

here!"

"It is rather, I can barely wait."

"I have been wandering around looking like a dog with two tails. The Boss, my friend, Andreas, has been giving me funny looks, can I tell him?"

"Tell him what we are going to be doing in Menorca?"

"No, that is for me to dream about." I feel my eyes starting to glaze over, I snapped myself out of reverie. "No, I was thinking more about how I have met the most beautiful, wonderful, woman to grace the planet; and that she finds it amusing to have me around!"

"Who is this woman? I'll scratch her eyes out!"

I laugh, then I said it.

"I love you, Soph!" Silence from the other end of the phone. Had I said the wrong thing? Panic started to rise in my chest. "Soph?"

"I… thank you!" Followed by something inaudible and a sob.

"Soph?"

"I said, I think I … I must go, I'll call you tomorrow." The phone went dead.

That almost inaudible something … I wasn't sure but was it "I love you too?" I desperately hoped so.

*****

"I see you have a personal travel agent now!" Andreas had a piece of fax paper in his hand, as he walked into my office, a big smirk across his face.

I looked at the fax, Apartments Miramar, Santo Thomas, Menorca, 1 bedroom apartment. 28th July, four nights. Then there was more news, seats on a charter flight from London 28th and back on the 1st August. At the bottom was a handwritten note.

"*I hope this is suitable, Soph xxx*"

"Yes!"

"My travel agent never sends me kisses, just a bill!"

"That, dear Andreas, is because your travel agent isn't the best-looking woman in the world!"

"No, she is about to become my wife, if all goes well with this incoming project!"

"You and Kate!" I was delighted for my friend.

"Yes, now you can tell me all about," he squinted at the bottom of the fax, "Squiggle?"

"Ah, Squiggle, she is the most …" I dumped the entire story about our meeting and 'almost' all about our picnic. Andreas was a very good friend; he didn't look at his watch for nearly an hour.

"I have to go; I am supposed to be checking on the early shift tomorrow." Andreas stood up and stretched. "You'll be seeing the midnight crew before they start?"

"Yes, I have plenty to keep me busy until then." We had a four-shift system working during the summer. Andreas and I had agreed that we would put in an appearance at the start of each new shift in the rotation.

I started on the Health and Safety returns for the last month, nothing too onerous, the new culture was paying off. I had a couple of risks noted in the register. I copied them over, along with the steps we had taken to minimise the potential for any identified problem occurring or causing harm.

There was a single, work-related injury, a driver had twisted his ankle jumping from his cab and landing awkwardly. 'Idiot', I thought as

I made a mental note to find out why he had jumped, rather than using the steps.

The phone rang, "Hi Sicker-hets-kontor." I gave my phonetic greeting. My Norwegian was still basic and that was as close as I got to, *Hei, Sikkerhetskontor.*

"Hi, Sicko, what does that mouthful mean!" Soph!

"Squiggles! How lovely to hear your voice."

"Squiggles?"

"Andreas couldn't make out your signature beyond the S, hence Squiggles, I rather like it!"

"It is better than 'Sicko' anyway!"

"*Sikkerhetskontor.*" I tried to pronounce it correctly. "Norwegian for Safety Office, which is where I am sitting, slaving deep into the late-night twilight."

"Twilight? Of course, the Land of the Midnight Sun, I had forgotten!"

"It is much better than the Land Where the Sun Never Rises, at least it is above freezing out there."

"Poor you, we are still in the twenties! It has been a great summer."

"Apart from last Sunday!"

"Last Sunday might just have been the best day ever!"

"Certainly, it was part of the best weekend of my life!" Was I coming on a bit heavy?

"I hope we get to make that a 'best so far'! Everything on the itinerary I sent OK for you?"

"Yes fine, absolutely brilliant, will you be there the whole time?"

"Uhuh! I might be an hour later arriving at the apartment, but the whole time!"

"Wonderful, how much do I owe you?"

"Nothing. I have put you down as my significant other. Free flights on ScotAir for their aircrew and their partners. The apartment is a trial from Baker's, I have to go to a presentation as part of the deal. That is why I will be late getting there on the first day."

The conversation wandered on for a bit longer. Then I remember this was on her phone bill. time to wind the call-up.

"You are wonderful, Squiggles, I am so looking forward to this time with you. You have thought of everything."

"More than you know, I know about the local beaches, I got the 'skinny' from the rep."

"You can show me when we get there."

"I will do my best!" A rather fruity chuckle emerges from the earpiece, I must have missed something.

"Good night Squiggles, I love you."

"I think I love you too, good night! Captain No-pants!" More chuckles as the phone was put down.

*****

The days passed in a regular, well-ordered procession. We phoned each other frequently. Squiggles became 'Squigs' and I became 'Soff' for some reason that amused her far more than calling me by something like her old nickname should have done. I'd even looked it up in my English-Norwegian dictionary, nothing.

"I fixed your tickets for the Oslo to London leg, not the best seats, but the best flight."

119

"How much?" I wasn't going to have her paying; I was the rich one.

"Partner Airline." That meant it was free. I could get to like having a girlfriend in the travel business.

*****

Gatwick was crowded, it was my first encounter with the place in high season. That is my excuse for not spotting Squigs until she stroked my thigh checking my seatbelt was properly fastened. That, and the fact I had never seen her in uniform before.

"A bit of alright that one!" The chap sat next to me observed, as she moved away. "Ouff!" The woman in the window seat's elbow caught him in the ribs.

I got my book out of my jacket pocket and settled to read. I didn't see Squigs during the flight; she must have been working in the rear of the cabin. Someone else delivered my drink and tray of grey chicken and over-sweet chocolate mousse.

At Mahon, they cracked open the doors and the Mediterranean light flooded into the cabin. "Not long now! Have a nice stay!" My special stewardess smiled as I descended the steps."

The coach drove twice around the island before reaching Santo Thomas. The Baker's Holidays rep guided me to the apartment and gave me a quick tour of the rooms.

"I hope you and Miss Hudson, will enjoy your stay! I'll see you at the welcome meeting tomorrow morning, I hope."

"Thank you, it looks wonderful, I'm sure we will be very comfortable."

"Good, any questions, the meeting starts at eleven."

I shut the door behind her, I somehow doubted that we would make it to her meeting. I went to explore. I leant on the wall of the top floor balcony and looked out over the sea. The sun was well on its way to the horizon.

In the kitchen, I found the fridge, it was stocked! I found a note on the work surface.

"*Welcome to the Miramar Apartments. The drinks and aperitif package you ordered are in the fridge and the cupboard above. Please enjoy your stay.*"

It was signed by The Management.

I pulled off my shirt, grabbed a beer and went out onto the balcony. I took a mouthful of beer and was about to settle when my Mum's words of wisdom returned. I went back into the apartment, pulled the bottle of sun-lotion, I'd bought in Gatwick, from my hand luggage, and began to slather it on. Trousers! I don't want them getting grease-stained. I wipe my hands and slip them off. I'll need to do my legs too. Sod it! I take my pants off too. Lotion up and return to my beer.

I might have dozed for a few minutes. I didn't hear the door open or anything else … Until,

"Soff, naked already!"

I reach out to take Sophia in my arms, she steps back.

"Mind my uniform, you might be greasy Soff, get me a beer while I join you."

I did as I was told and went to collect two St Miguel from the fridge.

"What is with the 'Soff' thing", I ask over my shoulder.

"You'll see!"

I fetched the beers.

"Clothe -s off, that's much better," A naked woman stepped into my arms, we kissed and, as predicted, missed the welcome meeting.

*****

"If we don't get up soon we are going to miss lunch too!" I put my watch back down. "Or shall we wait until dinner time to eat?"

"If we are just going to stay in bed all day, we might as well have gone to Brighton!" Squig threw back the covers. "I'm going to shower, make me a coffee!"

After having watched my dream lover walk to the bathroom, I did what I had been told. Coffee made; I took the cups out onto the balcony. It was hot, very hot. I was admiring the view of the sun glinting off the sea.

"There you are Soff, can you do my back for me?" A bottle of lotion was thrust into my hand.

"Do you want me to do your front too?"

"Best not, not if we are going to get lunch!" She took the bottle from me. "I had better do your back, it is starting to go pink!" I let her do my front too!

The coffee was nearly cold. I drank it anyway.

"I've put the beach gear in a bag, go and

get dressed!"

"I thought we were going for lunch!"

The vision in a turquoise dress, smiled, "Typical boy, if it isn't your willie it's your stomach that rules everything. Dress! Lunch! Beach! Move!"

I moved, I dressed and we went for lunch. A simple steak and chips for me. I discovered I was ravenous. Squigs had the house salad, I finished it for her!

Then we started for the beach, "I thought it was ..." I pointed down a street we were crossing.

"Yes, but we are not going there, just follow. Today I am in charge!" I chased to regain the few steps I had fallen back. I thought I caught her adding, "Tomorrow I might have lost my nerve", under her breath.

We settled into a steady shamble, pointing out the flowers, birds and passing boats to each other. We were walking along a cliff path, except the cliff was only a couple of feet tall. There were places where the water came up to the cliff and others where small patches of sand were filled with families.

Suddenly, we were on a much larger patch of sand, definitely a beach. There were couples and families spread out on the sand, playing in the sea, just like any beach.

"Over there!" Squigs pointed to a clear patch and started walking towards it. I hurried along.

She stopped, pulled the two towels out of the beach bag and threw them on the ground. Then she pulled her dress up over her head.

"Come on, Soff, I need to get in the water before I lose my nerve!"

I pulled my clothes off, I got it! Soff; clothes off! I grabbed her hand and we ran, naked, into the water.

*****

"I'm glad you enjoyed the afternoon, Squigs!" We were strolling back towards the town. The sun was still shining but it was losing intensity.

"You were right about the comfort thing!" She swished her dress about. "Do clothes always feel constricting afterwards?"

"I can't honestly say," I reply.

"I thought you were some sort of expert!"

125

"I have probably spent twice as much time on a bare beach as you." Then a thought trickled into my mind, "And exactly the same amount of time as you in the countryside!"

And so to bed, as Pepys put it, except we went via dinner!

*****

The next morning we were up earlier, I had a mission. I'd left 'Miss Hudson writing postcards,' as I said to the Baker's rep when I ran into her in the reception area. After making a rather tongue in cheek apology for missing her meeting her welcome meeting, I asked about car hire.

"If you want to see the island, you should join our coach trip; there are still spaces for this morning."

"As I say, Miss Hudson is writing postcards and we really want to do a bit of house hunting!"

"Ah, in which case…" and she directed me to a small office, next to the place we had eaten lunch.

*****

"I must have taken the wrong turning!" The road had narrowed, the hedges and walls were crowding in on the wing mirrors of the little, red Fiat 127. I hoped that there would be a gateway or something soon, otherwise I was going to be reversing for a long way.

"We can't go much further; I can see the sea!" The joy of being in the passenger seat, I was too busy trying to avoid the rocks in the roadway from where the walls were collapsing. Then I noticed what appeared to be a gateway ahead of us. I drove through, hoping for room to turn the car around.

There was stacks of room, we were in what looked like a farmyard. A few tumble-down outbuildings, a circular courtyard and a house. Not far beyond the house, the sea sparkled invitingly.

I stopped the engine, peace. No sounds of chickens or dogs, just the constant scratch-scratch of the cicadas. The air was fresh and clean, there was no odour of pigs nor goats nor fish. The windows were all shuttered; apart from a gentle breeze ruffling the leaves of a fig tree, there was no movement.

"Let's have a look around, maybe someone can tell us where we are, and how to get to Macaraleta." That was our planned destination for today; before I took a wrong turning.

We walked over to the front door and

127

knocked, to see if we could raise anybody. There was no response. Then Squigs found the board, that had fallen from a nail in the doorframe.

Se vende … For Sale with a phone number. The house was obviously deserted I decided.

"I bet that is the track that leads down to the sea." Squigs pointed. "I could do with stretching my legs."

I needed to move a bit too, the drive had left my shoulders tense. We followed the path through a dip between the rocks. Then all at once, we were standing on a small, sandy strand, the sunlight glinting off the water. We were near the top of a small cala, a few hundred metres from the open sea. Close to the mouth of the inlet, we could see a small village. There were several small boats pulled up on the beach, surrounded by what I took to be piles of fishing tackle.

Further up the beach, a dozen or so people were enjoying the sun and sea. Off the shore, several leisure boats and yachts bobbed at anchor. Between where we were standing and that small beach on the far side was a jumble of rocks and boulders.

"This is nice," Squigs observed, scanning around the vista. "We could have our picnic, here on the sand."

I set off back to the car to pick up our food and the beach bag. Apart from the wind rustled leaves and the cicadas, it was silent. I collected the beach bag from the boot and started back towards our beach. In the distance, I heard a motor starting, the slow, steady thump of a marine diesel. One of the boats was on the move. From the end of the path I could see one of the fishing boats heading out towards deep water, the sound receded. I looked around, the sand was deserted, where was Sophia? Then I saw her, swimming back across the inlet. A few minutes later she emerged, naked and dripping. I handed her a towel.

"What was the water like?" I enquired.

"Warm. I swam out to see if there was anything on this side of the water. As far as I can see, this is the only place you can get down to the water until you get around the headland."

"So pretty much a private beach!" I handed her the suntan lotion. "Do my back will you." I pulled off my T-shirt and shorts.

As soon as we were both protected, we tucked into lunch, enjoying a shared can of cola before it got too warm. We had another, still wrapped in a towel to keep it cool.

129

"I wonder what happened to the people who lived here?" Squigs mused.

"I suppose something must have changed for the worse, why would anyone leave this place?"

"The same reason you work in Norway, perhaps?" A smart cookie is Miss Hudson. It got me thinking.

"There is one way to find out, I'll call that number."

"You don't speak Spanish, Soff. That might be a problem."

"I'll find a way around that. Let's go for a swim."

*****

The rest of the holiday went by in a blur of beaches, meals and passion. I found a lawyer who spoke good English and put him on the case. Then we flew home. Squigs in her uniform and me strapped in my seat, turbulence over the mountains in the centre of France.

I got some admiring glances from the waiting passengers at Gatwick as we parted company at the gate for my flight back to the chill of Norway.

August 1976

"There's no point in asking if you are feeling refreshed. You look like the dog with two tails."

I just smirked.

"The girl from James' wedding?"

"The very one." I throw myself down in the chair opposite Andreas' desk. A smile as broad as the North Sea on my face.

"Good, you can tell me all about her another day. The helicopter is coming for me in an hour and we have a handover to do."

"A helicopter?" We had assurances that one was available for evacuating casualties. We had never used it. Now one was being sent for Andreas.

"They want me in London first thing tomorrow, it is the only way they can get me on the late flight."

It appears that this is the start of something very big. However, we only had time for a short handover of the Issues Log. All was in pretty good order. No accidents causing injury. Production was close to the target, a plant breakdown had cost half a day, but we were closing the gap. I had the controls; Andreas boarded his helicopter and was whisked away south.

*****

It was a tough few weeks, only lightened by the regular calls to and from Squigs. At the end of the first week, I got a phone call from the Spanish lawyer. He has made contact with the person selling the house on Menorca.

"It is a matter of Inheritance Law. The rules are very clear, if rather old fashioned." His English was slow and measured as if he was selecting every word for correct nuance. "The owner of the house has died and there is no direct succession. The man selling the property is a nephew. This has tax implications."

"What does that mean in practice?" I had no idea about Spanish Laws and tax.

The lawyer explained that because the man who had inherited the house was not a direct descendant, he would have to pay a huge amount of tax. However, if the house was up for sale, he could claim for maintenance, security and even decay during that period.

"As you have seen, the house is for sale, but not just yet. Next year, after the allowances had been claimed, if the price was right. Maybe the owner might sell." He finished the explanation.

I told him that I would be interested in buying the house, "if the price is right." We agreed to talk again before the end of the year and rang off.

*****

The good news for the month was the decision of Mr Sod not to invoke his law over the middle of the month.

Squigs had wangled a rota on the flights to Norway, covering for another girl's holiday. The thrice-daily flights meant an overnight stay in Oslo. She would arrive on the Thursday late flight and have to go back on the morning flight on Friday. Could I get to Oslo for the night?

Then Andreas called. He needed an update on the situation in Finnmark. He also wanted to talk about his future.

"You know I have been seeing Kate for a few years!" He added enigmatically. He knew that I knew they were planning to marry in the spring. He wanted to talk about something else, but not over the phone.

"How about next Thursday? You could come on the early flight, I could fly down,

133

although I might not get back until the following day. I'll book a room for us to meet anyway and if I am too late to fly back …"

"That works for me, I hope it does for you!" Andreas is nobody's fool.

*****

That had gone stunningly well. I was sitting in the plane heading north but I had the feeling I could have flown without one. It wasn't just the night of passion that had me buzzing.

I'd arrived at the hotel to meet with Andreas as planned. He was smiling. He took the notes I had prepared and put them in his bag.

"Anything in there that anybody might want to ask me questions about?"

"I don't think so, everything is on track to hit targets. We are ahead of the sun on the maintenance." We have a schedule that is designed to have all the maintenance on the site and equipment done before the cold hits in early September.

"Good, I'll read the notes on the way back." He looked around furtively. "Did you book a room? I don't want anyone to overhear us talking."

"The non-disclosure chat again?" I asked

"That and more."

I collected the room key and ordered coffee to be brought up. We walked up the stairs in silence. I opened the door; Andreas checked the corridor, looking both ways, before stepping inside the room.

"We have done good my friend, you and me both. Andreas has been working for you." He laughed, heartily. "Oh Yes! Andreas has been working hard for himself and for you!"

It transpired that we had done good, we had done very well indeed. The American owners had used our record in the North to convince the Regulators that they were fit and proper people to take over an ailing conglomerate with assets scattered across Britain and Europe.

Guess who were to be the acceptable, European faces of the new subsidiary this side of the Atlantic. Yes, their successful Norwegian team.

"We have to move away from the mine too!" Andreas was excited. "They wanted us to set up an office in London."

"Wanted?" I asked. I could see nothing

wrong with being back in the UK.

"Why London? It is crowded, noisy, dirty and very expensive. In London, we would be small players. Then Kate," Ah, yes the beautiful, *northern* belle. Emphasis on the northern. I might have guessed … "pointed out that 'the Man from London' is not a popular figure with the workers."

A very good point. Kate is not just a pretty face then. I remembered how my co-workers used to view the Managers from Oslo. I think the word for their attitude is contempt.

"So I managed to convince the Americans that I should be based in Leeds, part of the Yorkshire Coalfield." He winked. "Good international connections from Manchester and Leeds Airports. Trains and motorways to the rest of Britain. They bought it."

"Leeds? I suppose it is warmer than Tromso but not much!"

"You aren't going to Leeds!" Andreas laughed. "Andreas has been working for both of us. I am in Leeds with the lovely Kate. The management of USMM wants us in different places."

"What? Why different places?" I am confused.

Andreas paused, while the coffee was delivered.

Then he explained that while the Americans had accepted us being in charge of a small mine in the icy wastes of Arctic Norway, that acceptance extending to a pan-European conglomeration was not in their plans. That was the pressure from the European Coal and Steel Community who wanted to limit the American influence. So we are the figureheads, Europeans.

"Our masters don't want us getting too cosy though. I expect they will be keeping us on a shorter leash."

I had been surprised they had left us alone for so long. Waiting for us to fall on our faces so that they could rush in a Head Office Rescue Team, maybe. A group of trouble-shooters that would sort everything out, then never leave.

"I am to be based in the English mining areas because I am not English. You are to be based in the 'Group Safety Office' near Strasbourg, to show how keen our employers are on safety. These are political decisions, that is the world we are now inhabiting."

"How am I supposed to report to you, Andreas? We'll even be in different time zones!"

"That is another change, we now work to separate bosses. It goes well with our new titles; I am the Director of European Operations and report to the Director of Global Operations."

That sounded like Andreas was well on his way up the greasy pole!

"You, as the new Head of Safety Engineering, will report to the CEO of Corporate Affairs."

"A European CEO?" I ask, confused by the apparent newcomer in the structure.

"No the American guy, Schutz. You, my son, are going global!"

"I don't have the experience for that sort of role!" I start to panic.

"Maybe not, but you have a developed a model that does two things they want. Firstly, your Shift Safety Teams have prevented accidents from happening, am I right?"

I agreed, the Teams had been great at picking up potential problems before they became incidents. "The second?"

"Not so nice. They see it as being a strategy for moving responsibility for accidents from Head Office to the operational locality."

"I can see how that would work as far as public relations go, until some innovation is blocked by someone up the line." Suddenly, I can see this actually being a great way of pushing responsibility for the safety of the workforce right the way up to the CEO. A real safety culture, imposed from the top by dint of appointing me! "Then it becomes a problem for that Manager and his Managers."

The whole structure is there in my mind. The local people spot a problem that needs to be addressed and pass it upward, until someone with enough authority either does something about it or agrees to accept the risk and the responsibility for doing nothing.

"It is going to involve a lot of travel. Visits to America as well as Europe!" Andreas had taken my silence as a sign that I was unhappy.

"Sorry, I was lost in a dream about the future!" I reassure him. "I just hope I can get all this in place before they see through me!"

"I don't know about that, but there is a bit that I haven't told you."

"What's that?"

"The pay increase …"

*****

139

I was still smiling about that when Andreas got his taxi back to the airport.

"You seem extraordinarily happy to see me tonight," Squigs announced, as I put her down after almost crushing her in a welcoming hug.

"You are here, we have tonight and I have just had some wonderful news from Andreas. Yes, I am very happy with life right now!" I beamed back. "Which would you prefer, France or Germany?"

"For what?"

"A place for us to set up home!"

"You might need to start from the beginning, I think I need to be brought up to speed on the events of today."

I guided her to the restaurant, found a quiet table for two and started to bring her up to date. We had finished our dessert and the coffee had arrived when I reached the end of my explanation.

"So," she paused. I fretted about what Squigs was going to say. "When you asked if I'd prefer France or Germany."

"Yes?" I hated all these pauses.

"Were you asking me to come and live with you?"

The penny dropped with a great big thud! That while I had known what I was asking, I hadn't made it clear to Squigs.

"I'm sorry, I should have said, 'I want us to live together; if that is acceptable, would you prefer to live in France or Germany?"

"How come I get the choice?"

"Strasbourg was in Germany once upon a time and now is in France. It is right on the border; I could establish the 'office' in either country and claim it was in the Strasbourg area."

That made Squigs grin. Then again, maybe it was something else she had in mind.

Sept 1976

Plans have a strange way of going slightly awry. Not necessarily wrong, if Mr Sod is looking the other way. I have ended up the owner of a very nice little coastal house just outside Olso. In a place called Konglungen, I will probably never get to see it. I have, however, read the details that are being used to sell it. It sounds nice; if you like cold water sailing!

I had swapped houses with Andreas. Well, that's what the paperwork says. Andreas could have sold his summer house; it is in a popular area. Moved the money to England and bought his house in Ripponden in the normal manner. Then he looked at how much the banks wanted to do the exchange. He had phoned me.

"Do you still have all your savings in your English bank?" I had replied in the affirmative. "Would you be interested in buying a house, that you could swap for mine?"

I could see the wins for both of us. Andreas would get a better exchange rate and no fees to move the money. I would get my money out of the hands of the British Government. As a result, I bought my first house and sold it for the same price, never having set foot in it.

Now, I was about to sell my second house, I hadn't physically been within ten miles of this one either.

After it was sold, all my money would be back in the Swiss account. Now when Squigs gets a bit of time off we can go house hunting in Germany. I had done a bit of research and chatted with my new boss.

His advice was not to get too close to the offices of the European Coal and Steel Community. "Our office needs to be close enough that you can respond within the hour but not so close they expect us to be at their beck and call."

Offenburg looked good, so that was where we were going to start looking.

December 1976

I drove back from Germany for Christmas. I was amazed at the number of BMWs, big Fords and Opels on the ferry with weird numberplates. Then I worked it out, most of the British Army on the Rhine and a couple of RAF stations were on their way home too.

At home, my German registered Merc caused a stir amongst the local schoolboys. The steering wheel on the wrong side and the speedo that went up to two hundred and twenty drew lots of comments. If I heard one lad confiding in his mates, "Yeah, they are allowed to go that fast on the German motorways!" I heard a dozen. The speedo was in kilometers, even so, the one hundred and forty miles an hour it could indicate were well beyond the dreams of my humble 280 S.

I used the opportunity of a longer period to introduce Sophia, yes, I used her full name, to my parents. Which went very well. I think Mum was starting to despair of me ever finding a nice girl and settling down. From the fuss, she made of Squigs I suspect that all her fears had been dashed and her hopes fulfilled.

"I have told you about Sophia several times and I wrote about her in lots of letters!" I protested.

"Don't try to correct your Mother. You are wasting your breath." My Dad confided in a whisper. "Let's go down the pub and leave them to it!"

We got back a couple of hours later and they didn't seem to have missed us. Mum was sat next to Sophia on the sofa. They were sharing something amusing in a book on Mum's knee.

The photo album!

"You looked so cute in that canvas army bath playing with your toy boat." Squigs smiled up at me. That meant they had done the baby pictures, at least I hadn't been forced to sit there while they cooed over me, as a three-month-old, laying on the rug in front of the fire.

The good news was Mum was still smiling as Sophia stood up, "Would you like a cup of tea, Mum? I suppose this one will need one!"

"Yes please, dear, and you'd better make one for Dad too!"

We had only had a couple of pints; it wasn't as if we were swaying or anything.

"I'll give you a hand," I announce and

follow Squigs into the kitchen.

"You were such a cutie when you were little!" She giggled, as she released me from the clinch she had held me in as the kettle boiled.

"You mean I'm not now?"

"A cutie, but you are not so little now!" Her hand pressed the front of my trousers.

I am sure the bulge was still evident when I carried the tray of tea things into the lounge. It was still there when I was trying to get to sleep in my single bed.

Mum's little boy slept alone! Even if Squigs and I lived together when she managed to get time off in Germany.

We had decided to rent a flat, as well as the office premises. There was still a shortage of housing to buy. The prices were high and the choice limited. So, like many young German couples, we were renting while we looked for the perfect house to come on the market. It seemed to be working out fairly well so far.

There were signs that I wasn't going to be spending a lot of time in the office. I was expected in the States soon after Christmas for a series of meetings. Then there were all the

European mines and quarries to visit at least once. The very efficient Office Manager I had recruited to be a secretary before she promoted herself, would be running everything, while I was out galivanting.

"Galivanting?" I had queried Squigs choice of word.

"You should treat the first trip everywhere as a tourist trip because you'll be expected to hit the ground running when you go back." She had explained. "Try to get an insight into the local culture before you start making changes."

She was right, of course.

*****

I dropped Sophia back at the airport for her final shift before the holiday pause. Then I drove north, to meet up with Mr and Mrs Dec.

The door buzzed, I pushed it open and stepped in.

"You're early, Dec isn't back yet!" Mary called out. I followed the sound of her voice to the lounge.

"Good! It means I have a chance to beg you to run away with me. I have money, leave Dec he'll never find us!"

148

"You have a nerve! One letter from Norway, a postcard from Menorca and a change of address card in six months. If you wanted me that much, you'd have come sooner, besides Dec has your new address in his diary!" She hadn't lost her sense of humour. I leant forward over her chair and kissed her.

"You are still looking good, Mary. Are you and Dec coping?" The Cod War had ended in June, with a defeat for the British. The deep-sea fishing fleet was being scrapped as fast as the companies could get a price agreed.

"We are doing well, Dec has pulled off a stroke of genius that will keep us secure for several more years, but I'll let him tell you about it. A cup of tea?"

"Yes, please. Do you want me …" I bit my tongue; this was Mary's domain. It was not my place to take over. "… to come through with you?"

"No, just make yourself comfortable after your long drive." She pointed to an armchair. "I'll just be a few minutes."

The armchair was indeed comfortable. I took the chance to look around the simply furnished room. I suppose it was my professional eye that noted the little things. The wide doorway, the woven carpet, the space around the furniture and the absence of a tall bookcase. The room had been built to work with the restrictions of Mary's condition.

A few minutes must have passed because Mary was back, a tray of tea things balanced across her heavily modified wheelchair. The joy of being married to a practical engineer.

"Reading between the lines of your letter and the postcard, do I detect the signs of a significant other?" I didn't think I had been that obvious, then Mary is a sharp cookie.

"Yes, I think there is."

"The young lady from the wedding?" Mary's expression was beaming with delight. "Lindsey and I thought you might complement each other!"

So, it had been a stitch-up. The Bride and my friend's wife had been playing matchmakers.

"Once it was clear that Clive was in a worse way than me, it seemed the best thing to do. So tell me all about it!"

Over the next hour and two cups of tea, I brought Mary up to date with my love life. More than up to date, her gentle probing had made me look into corners of myself I had been ignoring.

Just as we were reaching the end of the conversation, well as far down the line as I was going to go! The front door opened, of course, it was Dec.

"It's great to see you, so how's your love life?"

I knew I should have waited until both of them had been in the room. I did find it much easier the second time around.

"That is brilliant. I'm glad to hear that you are settling down at last!" Dec announced, as I wound up reporting how the meeting with my parents had gone.

The wonderful thing was I was glad to hear that I was settling down.

"We thought we would get a curry and a few beers tonight. Mary likes to get out and I have reserved a table at one of the local restaurants."

"Sounds good to me Dec, but wouldn't a takeaway make it easier for you to have a beer?"

"Chauvinist! I will be doing the driving," Mary interrupted. "I'm not supposed to drink on my tablets! So, we always take my car!"

The curry had been most welcome, as had the few beers. Mary, as good as her word, had driven. The staff at the Kashmir Star had pushed out the boat to make her comfortable. It had been a great evening.

Mary had fetched a jug of water from the kitchen and pulled a bottle of Scotch out of a cupboard before declaring she was off to bed and, smiling broadly, asked us to keep it down.

"How is she doing?" I asked once Dec and I were alone with our whiskies.

"She gets very tired. She has been resting for several days in preparation for your visit."

As I thought, the days were slipping past for my friend and his wonderful wife. It made me more determined to make every hour with Sophia special.

We lapsed into quiet contemplation of our drinks.

"It's a single malt, from the Isles." Dec eventually broke the silence as he stood to fetch the bottle to refresh our glasses. "One of the skippers picked it up, they helped one of the local boats out of a bit of bother."

The ambiguity made it clear that no further details about the antecedence of our drink was of my concerned.

"Mary was saying that you have found a way through the current difficulties."

"Yes," we both looked into the clear amber fluid. "Fishing is over, they haven't read the last rites, but it will be gone in a few years. So, I set up on my own." The change in his mood was immediate. "I bought three of the smaller boats at the scrap price, had them modified and now two of them are standing as picket boats alongside oil production platforms. The third is in port for resupply ready to go out and replace one of them. Two at sea one in port or in transit all the time. I have bids in on another couple of boats and if I get the contract, they will serve the new Petroco platform as soon as it is taken out to sea."

Cod liver oil might now be a thing of the past but my friend had stayed in the oil business.

*****

I took my leave of Dec and Mary the following morning and drove south and west, heading for Sophia's family home. All this talking about her to other people was beginning to have me thinking of her by her proper name.

153

The Hudson's turn out to be a lovely couple. Her Dad, John, was as I had been warned, a bit eccentric and called me by a different name every time he spoke to me. "Cup of tea Tom?" or "a biscuit with that, Roger."

I didn't mind his teasing; I was too busy hoping the old saying about daughters turning into their mothers was true. Deborah Hudson was one of those graceful women who retain an ageless beauty. On the other hand, Soph's older brother is a bit of a plank, but it might just have been showing off.

With her brother home for the holidays, there was no room for me to stop over, so I had to head off home. I'd be back in a few days. Soph and I had been invited to Lindsey's parents New Year's Eve bash. A room had been booked at the George, so that was all taken care of. Christmas at home, then a few days later, I'd be back. Big brother would be skiing or something so there would be a bed for me.

"Drive safely and we'll see you on Wednesday then, Bartholemew!" John Hudson had called after me, as Soph walked me back to my car.

January 1977

The fireworks were still going off, I'd kissed more women in the last few moments than I had in … I couldn't work it out. It might have been the last party the old gang had before we all went our different way at the end of the sixth form!

Soph and I were the guests of Lindsey and James, who were home for the holiday period. He had been 'stood down' from his role at the Royal Engineers School in Kent for a couple of weeks.

Lindsey in particular was keen to know all about everything we were up to. It didn't take long for Soph to find out why. James' next posting was likely to be Germany. The British Army still had many thousands of men and lots of equipment based in the North to guard against an attack by the Warsaw Pact.

"It is a long way from Luneberg Heath to Strasbourg I point out, even on the Autobahn it would take hours to drive from one to the other's house!"

"It was just a thought." Lindsey looked disappointed. "I was just thinking it would be nice to have someone to visit when the boys are playing with their toys. Someone not 'army'." She added the last sentence in a conspiratorial whisper.

"As long as you realise it is an overnight trip, not just around the corner for coffee and cakes," Soph reassured her friend.

I was left wondering if I was the only one who could see the problem with this idea. The way things were working out, the chance of both Soph and me being home for longer than a day or two was going to be quite low for a while. We both had jobs that kept us on the move.

James and I left the women chatting and headed towards the bar, both of us selecting soft drinks when we got there. My drink of choice not being available I did an, 'I'll have the same' to whatever James had ordered. There was a lot of mixing and shaking and it tasted like orange juice with a bit of lemonade in it poured over lots of ice.

"A Harvey Wallbanger, but without vodka or the Galliano, I tip the bar staff for the performance and people don't question what I am drinking. A very useful ploy on formal mess nights, I can assure you."

We got separated when Lady Holstein-Hall grabbed James, "I need you to meet my cousin, she is from Australia and missed the wedding. She is dying to meet …"

I lost the rest of the story of the distant cousin as James was dragged away. I wasn't alone for long.

"There you are. my boy!" A voice boomed at me.

"My Lor … Henry! How are things going with the house? Have you had time to visit your pied-a-terre?"

"The purchase all went well, thanks to you. If I can ever return the favour, don't hesitate." We were interrupted by one of His Lordship's associates. I was suddenly an interloper in the conversation. He turned away from his contemporary, for a second, "Remember, anytime, don't hesitate!"

Strange how things can just drop into place, just like that.

Our taxi was due, I went and found Soph, we said our goodbyes to the Holstein-Hall's and the Hesketh-Stuarts. We had to wait for our coats but we were still in time for our driver to take us to the George.

*****

"Did I see you talking to Lord Rochester last night?" The George had delayed breakfast

157

to a civilised hour. The full English had been an absolute delight. I was enjoying a second cup of tea, when Soph's question unlocked the thought that was trapped in my mind.

"Yes, he is grateful for the service I was able to do him! The house purchase went through." I take a sip from my cup. "It reminded me about that place on Menorca. I was just thinking I ought to ring that lawyer chap, see if the seller has had any thoughts about what he wants to do."

"Can we afford two houses, Germany and Menorca?"

"No, but then I have a well-paid job in Germany, getting a mortgage on a place there wouldn't be that difficult." We had never had a conversation about money, beyond who was going to pay for a meal out.

"I could contribute too; I get almost three hundred pounds a month. Senior Cabin Crew get a pretty good deal!"

"I get a little more than that, my miner's salary has been more than doubled since I came in from the freeze." I am slightly embarrassed by how much I am earning. "I get paid in dollars, after it gets converted I get some six thousand marks a month." I watch her doing the sum in her head.

"That's about fifteen hundred pounds a month!" She hisses across the table to me.

"Uhuh, three hundred a week give or take." I didn't want to get into the bonuses that I'll be getting four times a year, unless there is some sort of major accident.

"Wow, not only do I have a ruggedly handsome boyfriend but I now discover he is rich too!"

"No, I'm not rich. I am well paid and one day, with luck, *we* will be rich!" I reach out, across the table and take her hand and squeeze it gently. "*We* will be rich."

*****

The rest of the month went by in a blur. Between trips to the mines the company now operated in Europe and a couple of trips to America, I did manage to get the Spanish lawyer on the case about the house.

Generally, I was welcomed by the managers of the European mines, many of whom had been left worried by the American acquisition of the former owners. They were scared of the idea that the 'bottom line' was all that would matter in the future.

In the American plants, I was viewed as some kind of 'Commie' looking to empower the

159

workers to challenge management over the running of the industry. "We all know what your unions have done to industry over in England!" And variations of this theme met me everywhere.

I tried to explain that as I saw it, "Fewer accidents meant less interruption to production; which in turn would generate better profits!" In general, they weren't listening. I suspected that someone had turned them against me. This was going to be a hard sell!

April 1977

The house on Menorca was ours. The sale had been pretty painless once we had found a way of minimising inheritance tax for the chap selling it. The way it had been arranged we had paid him several commissions, a finder's fee, a commission for introducing a surveyor, the builders to do some remedial work and such like. These extras were taken off the sale price. It hadn't made a lot of difference to the tax he was paying as far as I could see, but it kept him happy and we were content with the price.

When we arrived for our first stay at the house we were delighted to have made it. Soph had been struck down with Delhi-belly during a flight to Madeira. She was too ill to fly back and had spent several days on the toilet in a hotel in Funchal. She was still feeling a little bit fragile when we flew into Mahon.

Her low energy matched the spring weather, grey, dank and cool. As she recovered, the weather improved and we moved from the house to the terrace outside and finally to our private beach.

In a way, I was glad that Soph was able to take her time recovering. Whatever it was had hit her hard. If she had been back at work, she would have put her all into it and probably over-done it.

The other good thing was we got to live in the house. It gave us food for thought. After dinner on the second or third night, we started doodling how we could remodel the house before we redecorated and bought 'our' furniture. It was initially just a fun game. Then we had to pause going upstairs to bed. Soph had pushed her limits washing up and needed to regroup.

"We need to look at those ideas again." I was getting into bed when it struck me. "You struggled up the stairs, imagine our parents, five or ten years from now; will they be wanting to climb the stairs?"

"Or even able to climb the stairs, accidents and other health problems can happen at any time!" Soph caught on quickly to my train of thought. "As it is we couldn't have Dec and Mary to stay."

"… *I fell in love with it when … I was fourteen and had never visited anywhere so beautiful. I know it won't be the same in December but I want to share it with Dec*" Mary had said to me at their wedding. It was why I had come to the island and fallen in love with it myself. That was when the doodles became serious.

We moved the lounge from the ground floor to the first floor. In fact, the views from the big windows of that bedroom and the balcony were stunning; not that we foresaw it being used much in summer. There would still be a large bedroom for us, with access to the balcony. The two other bedrooms and the family bathroom and the toilet would stay as they were.

"It would be good to have a small private bathroom just for us, like in the hotels," Soph suggested. I drew it in the corner of our room, next door to the main bathroom.

Downstairs, we turned what had been the lounge into a 'guest suite' modelled on the room I had been assigned in Las Vegas.

"Doorways, they will need to be wider than normal!"

"Ones like the saloon doors in the westerns, double doors that swing open both ways! Or sliding doors that pull open wide."

"Patio doors! so that they can get in and out of the house on the level!" Soph was well into this.

The new ground floor guest accommodation, now exited onto the rear terrace. There was going to be a large, open plan shower room. A double door was

163

sketched in for access to the dining room and kitchen beyond.

"Now all we need is the money and a reliable builder to do the work!"

The money was not going to be a problem. The first quarter of the year had been remarkable. Not a day lost to accidents anywhere in Europe and only three had been lost in the USA. I still hadn't fully explained how my bonuses were calculated to Soph. Nor had I specified how large they could be. After all, they could be lost more easily than won. I remember my Dad's commission payments drying up and leaving the family finances very tight not so long ago!

Finding reliable workmen, that was going to be a trick!

"My brother."

"Your brother? What about your brother, Soph?"

"This sort of thing is what Paul does. He has a team of guys he works with; they do refurbishments and convert houses into flats."

"Is he good?"

"I think so, Dad wouldn't risk his reputation if he wasn't."

I was lost, I realised I knew nothing about the Hudson family. I was forced to admit my lack of knowledge and ask.

"Dad is a Master Builder; he has run his own company for as long as I can remember. Mum's parents were architects and she took over the practice when they retired. Between them, they have a reputation for creating the best houses in the county. Paul was supposed to take over the firm but he decided that working in freezing, muddy trenches or being blown off scaffolds was not for him. He moved on to doing interiors, basics at first, but they are now doing special finishes for Mum and Dad."

"I have been here doodling plans, making decisions about a wall here and a door here, and your Mum is an architect?" My opinion of the glamourous Deborah Hudson ratcheted up a couple of notches.

"She likes it when people have definite ideas about what they want. She says it is easier to cook chips for someone than to cook samples of every type of potato dish for them to choose from!"

"Proper plans? She would need to get the place properly measured surely?"

"And Paul would need to see the environment and what is available by way of

165

materials and equipment."

"Do a proper estimate for us too." My bonus was considerable but there is a limit to my money.

"I can arrange to be here with them while you are in the States next week."

"Do you think they would consider doing this for us?"

"They will be happy to do it, my contribution to the purchase."

We went out to eat that evening.

*****

The following week I was on a plane to New York, as the passengers were being called forward to be boarded, I noticed Lord Rochester ahead of me in the queue. We are sat on opposite sides of the aisle. I decided I should be the one to make an acknowledgement of the other's presence.

"Good morning, My Lord." I smile. He double-takes. I expect he wasn't expecting to see me on a Concord flight. "The Corporation I work for values my time and saving a day travelling appears to make sense to them," I explain in response to the unasked question that followed the exchange of greetings.

"Hmm, that contradicts what I was told about you, someone told me you were a miner in Norway."

"I was at the time, then things changed," I explain the way my role had changed in fairly short order. This was the first time had explained my scaling of the corporate ladder. I was horrified when I heard it. I realise I had gone from spotty student to a man who flies on Concord, via a spade and thick anorak, in just a few years.

"So you are the new safety hot shot at US Mineral Extractions? The one everybody is waiting to see crash and burn?" His Lordship seems well informed.

"I was part of the deal that got them the permits to operate in Europe," I reply somewhat coyly.

"Well, whatever you do it seems to be working." Make that His Lordship seems *very* well informed.

"The Americans don't seem to be as willing to take to my ideas."

"I have heard you being called a Commie who wants to allow the Unions to close places down if they don't like the look of the weather!" Where was His Lordship getting this information? And, just as importantly, why?

167

"I have had Union Chiefs saying I am the boss' stoolie, sent in to reduce the 'danger money' they get paid. 'If we are making the place safe, we don't need to be paid so much!' Or some such rubbish."

"Luck with getting anywhere against that sort of opposition."

"I hope you remember that offer you made back at New Year, Henry! I may need to call on you sooner rather than later." I tried to laugh but didn't pull it off with any conviction.

"Of course, Young Man, call me when you are ready. You still have my private number?"

What was going on here?

Before I could ask any more questions, the smoking light went out and the seat belt one came on. The hostesses started bustling backwards and forwards with last orders, tidying the debris away while fending off propositions and proposals from some of the passengers. I wondered if Soph had to put up with the same sort of treatment.

*****

We landed at JFK in New York; Lord Rochester was VIP'ed off to some private lounge for the emigration formalities. I joined the queue to be scowled at and have my passport stamped by an officious man in a uniform.

From that point, things were to head downhill far faster than I had expected. I was treated politely and granted every courtesy. I just wasn't allowed to do anything. I wasn't allowed to present my ideas. I wasn't allowed to visit any of the facilities without an escort. Even then, I got the distinct impression other people were being steered out of my path.

A week later, I had it all worked out. I had just had a debriefing meeting with the bosses. I had enough meeting experience to work out how the points they were making would appear in the minutes.

They were playing me for a fall guy. I was being set up to fail. They weren't going to change anything. There would be an incident, the Head Honcho in safety would be deemed to have failed. His new ideas had not prevented people from being killed or injured and production lost.

As the Head of Safety Engineering, I was that Head Honcho. My boss, the CEO of Corporate Affairs, would be protected. 'The guy was foisted on us by the Europeans.'

On the flight home, I decided that with Soph's agreement, I would resign before they could sack me.

Soph didn't agree.

"I have been reviewing my recordings of our meeting, put in the time and date there," Soph dictated as I wrote. "My interpretation of what was said suggests that you are currently trying to manoeuvre me into an unsustainable position. There are risks to both of us in this strategy." New paragraph. "I would like to propose that it might be mutually beneficial if suitable terms for my resignation could be agreed upon."

"But I don't have a recording of the meeting." I point out the weakness in the letter.

"You know that. I know that. Can they be sure you haven't?"

May 1977

Before I sent that first letter to America, I phoned Lord Rochester. 'It's not just who you know but how you use them.' It was one of my father's pet sayings. It had served me well when I had used Andreas' contacts to get a job and move ahead. Andreas had pushed his willingness to help onto me, unasked.

I had another invitation to ask anytime, and it had been repeated. I picked up the phone and dialled the number from the back pages of my diary.

This time I was passed through to His Lordship very smoothly. It was as if my call was expected.

"I am impressed with the speed you have acted, My Boy!" As if my call … "I thought you might try to push ahead for a few more months. I am pleased to hear you didn't."

"You said to call."

"My office, Tuesday at … midday. No, make it half-past eleven. We can lunch if it looks like we need more time."

"Thank you, my Lord."

"Henry!"

"I was practising for next week."

"Smart, careful you don't cut yourself. Tuesday!"

*****

A traffic accident blocked the road out of Dover, it delayed me by a couple of hours. By the time I reached my parents' house, the library was closed. I had planned to make a quick trip to the reference section to look up Lord Rochester's entry in Who's Who.

I was still very much in the dark when I arrived at the prestigious looking building that matched the address Henry had given me. The Head Office of British Minerals, Metals and Ores Traders. That at least explained how, if not why, Henry was aware of my role with USMM.

Henry wheeled me into what I had to assume was the Board Room. It wasn't a formal meeting but business was being discussed in groups of two, three or four men. Every so often, someone would move from one group to another.

"This is our regular information exchange meeting. So much of mining is controlled by big conglomerates, as you know, one of the Houses, say gold, may know about an issue in a mine in Bolivia. Not a big concern for us in itself you might think. However, gold production uses a lot of mercury. Gold of course is globally important.

"By having these little chats, that sort of gossip gets spread around and the House looking after our business in mercury get to hear earlier than they otherwise would." Lord Rochester explained the rationale to me as we moved from group to group. I was introduced to lots of people and asked a few questions. Sometimes they were about me, others were quite technical about the continuity of supply of bauxite from USMM.

"We do what it says on the tin," Lord Rochester explained over lunch. I must have passed some sort of test at that exchange meeting. The way the word 'we' was being used suggested I was part of 'we'. "We are a brokerage, we buy metals, minerals and ores on behalf of manufacturers and processors here in Great Britain and increasingly around the world. We buy in bulk, getting a good price then sell them on to our customers." We paused while our food was served. It was the first time I had been into a Gentleman's Club.

"The whole of the Industrial West has been caught out a few times when the production of key resources has been forced to stop." He continued, while I attacked my steak. "In the past, when something went wrong, we have had to scrabble around looking for alternative suppliers. That is us, along with everyone else, trying to source something exotic, like tantalum, when the one mine we all use stops work. That pushes prices up, profits down and our customers hate it."

"This is all very interesting Henry, but where do you see me fitting in?"

"We, I, thought your specialism could be of considerable help in mitigating against these risks."

"How?"

"I, We," I was getting an impression that Lord Rochester was British Minerals, Metals and Ores Traders personified. "Would like you to be our Mine Safety Consultant. To go out there, talk to the mine managers, use your eyes and come back and tell us which mines are 'a disaster waiting to happen'. Which are investing in ensuring continuity of production and which are already ahead of the game. That way we can secure our defensive positions with alternative suppliers before we need them."

"It is an interesting proposal, My Lord." Business, formal names! "How would you see the role working on a day-to-day basis?"

174

"I would imagine a few days 'up country', as the military wallahs used to say, snooping around, back to base for a week or so creating your report and any recommendations. We would be packing you off to the worst cases first, may be twenty operations a year." He pushed his dessert bowl away and wiped his mouth on a napkin. "How does that sound to you?"

"A good starting point. As long as I can adjust it as time passes and our experience goes up."

"Sensible, I leave this with you. If it is acceptable, give my PA a call and we will arrange a start date."

I put pen to paper and wrote the letter that Soph and I had composed a week ago. I put it in the post and went to the office to wait for the response.

They offered a year's salary.

At Lord Rochester's suggestion, I demanded, and got, an additional sum equivalent to my estimated bonus payment for June and September. In exchange, they got a letter of resignation that cited the constant travel between the United States and my base in Germany as the reason for leaving.

I officially left USMM on the thirty-first of

May. I hadn't done much work in that last month. I had, however, spent a lot of time in the office. Locked in, I was equipped with a couple of reams of paper and a replacement cartridge for the photocopier. I didn't want my ex-employers knowing how much of their confidential stuff I held in reserve. Just in case.

It was Andreas' idea. He had ordered a second photocopier for his office, on a personal contract, that he could use for backup copies. "There will be no trail they can follow!" He had laughed. "I'm sure they'll be coming for me soon!"

Andreas had little to fear from 'Early Retirement.' As a General Manager with experience at a high level for a 'Multi-National' business, doors would open for him. Unless someone set about blackening his reputation. That would have turned into a very messy spat, based on the papers he was making copies of.

Unlike my situation, he could afford a break from work too. His father had made a lot of money out of the sale of the Norwegian mine.

I won't be starting the new job until July. A whole month off and the work in Menorca had just been completed.

Just as well, I had started to think Soph might have some sort of recurrence of her stomach bug. She had been sent home from work three days running and told to go and see the doctor. Neither of us is confident of our ability to understand the special German a doctor would use. We left it a couple of days; we had planned to drive back to England to see our families before going to Spain.

June 1977.

I am enjoying the feel of sunshine on my back.
I am lying on a towel spread out on a sandy
beach in Menorca. I decide to turn over before
I burn. I still enjoy the fabulous feeling of being
warm, without layer upon layer of clothing.

For over two years, I had worked in the
Arctic North. Norway to be precise, north of the
city of Tromso; one of the most hostile
environments in the world. Permanent
darkness, from mid-November to mid-January.
Cold, between October and April it seldom gets
above freezing and it can get down to minus
eighteen degrees Celsius. The nearest city
was Soviet Murmansk. It wasn't as if you could
just pop over the border few a few days R and
R.

After that, the winter in Germany had
seemed mild. The Germans had complained
that it was colder than normal. Certainly, it had
seemed milder when I had been in England at
Christmas.

This is what had inspired me to spend
years in that freezing hell-on-Earth. The dream
of being able to afford to be lying on this
beach. To be able to watch some hippy chicks
scrambling on the rocks and playing in the sea

179

without a care in the world, and even fewer clothes. While I wait for the most wonderful woman in the world to bring me a fresh, cold, beer.

Meeting James on his doorstep that distant day in Leeds had been the start of it all, I realise. James excepting me to share his house. Then Dec arriving to take the second room. The Grimsby lad, who had, in turn, brought his friend Andreas into my life.

James' advice about targets had helped to get me through the early days in the icy wilderness. That tough times when you are alone, homesick, frozen to the bone and trying to survive in a hostile environment.

It was Captain James Hesketh-Stuart's invitation to his marriage to Lindsey Holstein-Hall that made the biggest difference though. After all, it was at the wedding that I had met my new career mentor and most important of all, Sophia Lauren Hudson.

"Speak of the devil!" A shadow had fallen over me.

"You weren't speaking and if I was the devil, I'd have poured this cold beer over you!"

"My mistake my Angel, I thought you were someone else." I fib as I sit up, reaching out to take both cans from her. I take a sip of my beer, while she gets comfortable on the towel. I hand her the can of cola.

"I see," Soph is looking across the inlet to where the hippies are trying to catch prawns. "It was one of those naked nymphs you were thinking of!"

"Not at all, I only have eyes for you." I am not fibbing this time.

"Well, best enjoy it while you can, Dec and Mary arrive in a couple of hours. We will both have to dress to go to the airport."

"Then I suppose it will be clothes for the rest of the week." I regard Soph, sitting in the sun, holding her cola against her brow. "I hadn't realised how quickly one gets used to being bare all day."

"It might not be that bad." She sipped from her can of cola.

"What do you mean, Soph?"

"I phoned Mary just before we flew here, to check everything was sorted with the airline for her. We talked about the house being a considerable distance from any medical facility. She said that she felt well and they would cross that bridge if the need arose."

"Very philosophical at times is Mary, I

suppose that comes with knowing." I stopped talking, Soph's face told me I had interrupted.

"I also mentioned the beach and how private it is. She asked if it would be good for skinny dipping. She goes on to tell me that one of the things on her, 'You Only Live Once' list is to swim naked in the ocean. At that, I mentioned about your choice of sunbathing wear. That created a bit of excitement, she has added, spend a whole day naked to her list!"

"And how does Dec feel about this?"

"I get the feeling he doesn't know, or at least he didn't before they got on the plane." She giggled. I imagined Mary and Lindsey had giggled just like that when they saw me escorting Soph on to dance floor at the wedding.

"That'll be interesting." I can't think of anything else to say.

"We had better get some stuff on your back, it is starting to get pink!"

"Or we could go up to the house and have a lie down for a while before going to meet them."

"We could!"

I leap to my feet, "Would you like a hand

up?"

"I'm not that fat … yet!"

I look at Soph's beautiful, naked figure. No, it doesn't look any different yet. That will come. The doctor, who had done the test, had explained that a bout of diarrhoea and vomiting could make the pill less effective…

ABOUT THE AUTHOR

Edward Yeoman was born in South London too many years ago. He was educated at Gillingham Grammar and the University of Kent. Where he obtained a very useful degree in Microbiology.

After spending years pursuing what is now called a 'portfolio career;' he retired. He now lives in a small house in the South of France with his wife Valerie. It is here he discovered what he really wanted to do in life and writes, mainly in the guise of Ted Bun.

Edward Yeoman has published several short stories and one other novel **"The Last Day of June."**

Being different I can't decide what genre that book belongs in either; any suggestions would be most welcome!

Follow my blog at   www.tvhost.co.uk
Facebook   www.facebook.com/ted.bun
Twitter   @Mr_Ted_Bun

Writing as Ted Bun

Rags to Riches Novellas

The Uncovered Policeman
The Uncovered Policeman Abroad
The Uncovered Policeman: In and Out of the Blues
The Uncovered Policeman: Goodbye Blues
Two Weddings and a Naming
The Uncovered Policeman: Caribbean Blues
The Uncovered Policeman: Family Album
A Spring Break at L'Abeille Nue
The Uncovered Policeman: Made for TV
The Uncovered Policeman: The Long Road
The Uncovered Policeman: Live, Laugh and Love
The Uncovered Policeman: A New Home in the Sun
While Bees Sleep

Rags to Riches Short Stories

The Cutters' Tale
The Naked Warriors
The Girls Trip to the Beach
Cocoa and Pyjamas
Forty Shades of Green
BareAid
The Uncovered Policeman's Casebooks

Other Novellas

New House … New Neighbours

New House … New Address
New House … New Traditions

The Summer of '71 (A Crooke and Loch story)
Runners and Riders (A Crooke and Loch story)
The Summer of '76 (A Crooke and Loch story)

Problems and Passions (NBL Solutions 1)
Problems of Succession (NBL Solutions 2)
Problems in the Pyrenees (NBL Solutions 3)

The Day Before Last

When the Music Stops: DC al Fine
Then Play On

The Girl with a Ginger Cat

Other Short Stories
Going South – Forever
The Dancer
A Job in the City
New Laws
When the Music Stops

Printed in Great Britain
by Amazon